TRAS

D0447096

Spaceship from Earth:

As it came within eye range, it loomed vast in the glare of the distant yellow-white sun, bigger than anything ever seen by the Fifty Suns. It seemed a very hell ship out of remote space, a monster from a semi-mythical world, and—though a newer model—recognizable from the descriptions in the history books as a battleship of Imperial Earth. Dire had been the warnings in the histories of what would happen some day —and here it was.

So begins A. E. van Vogt's suspense-filled story of the far-distant future . . .

mission
to the stars

(Originally published as THE MIXED MEN)

A. E. van VOGT

A BERKLEY MEDALLION BOOK
published by
BERKLEY PUBLISHING CORPORATION

Published by arrangement with the author's agent

BERKLEY EDITION, NOVEMBER, 1956
2nd Printing, November, 1957
3rd Printing, January, 1958
BERKLEY MEDALLION EDITION, NOVEMBER, 1962
(4th Printing)
5th Printing, September, 1963
6th Printing, March, 1971 (New Edition)

SBN 425-01973-X

This book is based upon previously published stories by A. E.
van Vogt: "Concealment" and "The Storm," copyright 1943
by Street and Smith Publications, Inc., and "The Mixed Men,"
copyright 1945, by Street and Smith Publications, Inc.

BERKLEY MEDALLION BOOKS are published by
Berkley Publishing Corporation
200 Madison Avenue
New York, N. Y. 10016

BERKLEY MEDALLION BOOKS ® TM 757,375

Printed in the United States of America

Prologue

THE Earth ship came so swiftly past the planetless Gisser sun that the alarm system in the meteorite weather station had no time to react. The great ship was already visible as a streak of light on the observation screen when Watcher grew aware of it. Alarms must have been activated in the ship, also, for the moving point of brightness slowed noticeably and, evidently still braking, made a wide turn. Now it was creeping slowly back, obviously trying to locate the small object that had affected its energy screens.

As it came within eye range, it loomed vast in the glare of the distant yellow-white sun, bigger than anything ever seen by the Fifty Suns. It seemed a very hell ship out of remote space, a monster from a semi-mythical world, and —though a newer model—recognizable from the descriptions in the history books as a battleship of Imperial Earth. Dire had been the warnings in the histories of what would happen some day—and here it was.

He knew his duty. There was a warning, the age-long dreaded warning, to send to the Fifty Suns by the nondirectional subspace radio; and he had to make sure that nothing telltale remained at the station. There was no fire. As the overloaded atomic engines dissolved, the massive building that had been a weather substation simply fell into its component elements.

Watcher made no attempt to escape. His brain, with its knowledge, must not be tapped. He felt a brief, blinding spasm of pain as the energy tore him into atoms.

The Lady Gloria Laurr, Grand Captain of the Star

Cluster, did not bother to accompany the expedition that landed on the meteorite. But she watched with intent eyes through the astroplate. From the very first moment that the spy rays had shown a human figure in a weather station —a weather station *out here*—she had known the surpassing importance of the discovery. Her mind leaped instantly to the several possibilities.

Weather stations meant interstellar travel. Human beings meant Earth origin. She visualized how it could have happened: an expedition long ago; it must have been long ago because now they had interstellar travel, and that meant large populations on many planets. His majesty, she thought, would be pleased.

So was she. In a burst of generosity, she called the energy room. "Your prompt action, Captain Glone," she said warmly, "in inclosing the entire meteorite in a sphere of protective energy is commendable, and will be rewarded."

The man whose image showed on the astroplate bowed. "Thank you, noble lady. I think we saved the electronic and atomic components of the entire station. Unfortunately, because of the interference of the atomic energy of the station itself, I understand the photographic department was not so successful in obtaining clear prints."

The woman smiled grimly as she said, "The man will be sufficient, and *that* is a matrix for which we need no prints." She broke the connection, still smiling, and returned her gaze to the scene on the meteorite.

As she watched the energy and matter absorbers in their glowing gluttony, she thought: There had been several storms on the map in that weather station. She'd seen them in the spy ray; and one of the storms had been very large. Her great ship couldn't dare go fast while the location of that storm was in doubt.

He had seemed rather a handsome young man in the flashing glimpse she had had in the spy ray. Strong-willed, brave. Should be interesting in an uncivilized sort of fashion. First, of course, he'd have to be conditioned, drained of relevant information. Even now, a mistake might make it necessary to begin a long, laborious search.

Decades could be wasted on these short distances of a few light years, where a ship couldn't get up speed and where it dared not maintain velocity, once attained, without exact weather information.

She saw that the men were leaving the meteorite. Decisively, she clicked off the intership communicator, made an adjustment and stepped through a transmitter into the receiving room half a mile distant.

The officer in charge came over and saluted. He was frowning. "I have just received the prints from the photographic department. The blur of energy haze over the map is particularly distressing. I would say that we should first attempt to reconstruct the building and its contents, leaving the man to the last."

He seemed to sense her disapproval, continued quickly: "After all, he comes under the common human matrix. His reconstruction, while basically more difficult, falls into the same category as your stepping through the transmitter in the main bridge and coming to this room. In both cases there is dissolution of elements—which must be brought back into the original solution."

"But why leave him to the last?" she asked.

"There are technical reasons having to do with the greater complexity of inanimate objects. Organized matter, as you know, is little more than a hydro-carbon compound, easily conjured."

"Very well." She wasn't as sure as he that a man and his brain, with the knowledge that had made the map, was less important than the map itself. But if both could be had—She nodded with decision. "Proceed."

She watched the building take shape inside the large receiver. It slid out finally on wings of anti-gravity, and was deposited in the center of the enormous metal floor. The technician came down from his control chamber shaking his head. He led her, and a half dozen others who had arrived, through the rebuilt weather station, pointing out the defects.

"Only twenty-seven sun points showing on the map," he said. "That is ridiculously low, even assuming that these people are organized for only a small area of space.

And besides, notice how *many* storms are shown, some considerably beyond the area of the reconstituted suns and—" He stopped, his gaze fixed on the shadowy floor behind a machine twenty feet away.

The woman's eyes followed his. A man lay there, his body twisting. "I thought," she said frowning, "the man was to be left to the last."

The scientist was apologetic. "My assistant must have misunderstood. They—"

The woman cut him off. "Never mind. Have him sent at once to Psychology House, and tell Lieutenant Neslor I shall be there shortly."

"At once, noble lady."

"Wait! Give my compliments to the senior meteorologist and ask him to come down here, examine this map, and advise me of his findings."

She whirled on the group around her, laughing through her even, white teeth. "By space, here's action at last after ten dull years of surveying. We'll rout out these hide-and-go-seekers in short order."

Excitement blazed inside her like a living force.

The strange thing to Watcher was that he knew before he wakened why he was still alive. Not very long before. He *felt* the approach of consciousness. Instinctively, he began his normal Dellian preawakening muscle, nerve and mind exercise. In the middle of the curious rhythmic system, his brain paused in a dreadful surmise.

Returning to consciousness? *He!*

It was at that point, as his brain threatened to burst from his head with shock, that the knowledge came of how it had been done. He grew quiet, thoughtful. He stared at the young woman who reclined on a chaise lounge near his bed. She had a fine, oval face and a distinguished appearance for so young a person. She was studying him from sparkling gray eyes. Under that steady gaze, his mind grew very still. The thought came, finally: "I've been conditioned to an easy awakening. What else did they do—find out?" The thought grew until it seemed to swell his brainpan: WHAT ELSE?

He saw that the woman was smiling at him, a faint

amused smile. It was like a tonic. He grew even calmer as the woman said in a silvery voice: "Do not be alarmed. That is, not too alarmed. What is your name?"

Watcher parted his lips, then closed them again, and shook his head grimly. He had the impulse to explain then that even answering one question would break the thrall of Dellian mental inertia and result in the revelation of valuable information. But the information would have constituted a different kind of defeat. He suppressed it, and once more shook his head.

The young woman, he saw, was frowning. She said: "You won't answer a simple question like that? Surely your name can do no harm."

His name, Watcher thought, then what planet he was from, where the planet was in relation to the Gisser sun, what about intervening storms. And so on down the line. There wasn't any end. Every day that he could hold these people away from the information they craved would give the Fifty Suns so much more time to organize against the greatest machine that had ever flown into this part of space.

His thought trailed. The woman was sitting up gazing at him with eyes that had gone steely. Her voice had a metallic resonance as she said: "Know this, whoever you are, that you are aboard the Imperial Battleship *Star Cluster*, Grand Captain Laurr at your service. Know too, that it is our unalterable will that you shall prepare for us an orbit that will take our ship safely to your chief planet."

She went on vibrantly: "It is my belief you already know that Earth recognizes no separate governments. Space is indivisible. The universe shall not be an area of countless sovereign peoples squabbling and quarreling for power. That is the law. Those that set themselves against it are outlaws, subject to any punishment which may be decided in their special case. Take warning."

Without waiting for an answer, she turned her head. "Lieutenant Neslor," she said at the wall facing Watcher, "have you made any progress?"

A woman's voice answered: "Yes, noble lady. I have

set up an integer based on the Muir-Grayson studies of
colonial peoples who have been isolated from the main
stem of galactic life. There is no historical precedent for
such a long isolation as seems to have obtained here, so
I have decided to assume that they have passed the static
period, and have made some progress of their own. I
think we shall begin very simply, however. A few forced
answers will open his brain to further pressures; and we
can draw valuable conclusions meanwhile from the speed
with which he adjusts his resistance to the brain machine.
Shall I proceed?"

The woman on the chaise lounge nodded. There was
a flash of light from the wall facing Watcher. He tried
to dodge, and discovered for the first time that *something* held him in the bed. Not rope, or chain, or anything visible. But something as palpable as rubbery steel.

Before he could think further, the light was in his eyes,
in his mind, a dazzling furious vibratory thing. Voices
seemed to push through it, voices that danced and sang,
and spoke into his brain, voices that said:

"A simple question like that—of course I'll answer . . .
of course, of course, of course—My name is Gisser
Watcher. I was born on the planet Kaider III, of Dellian
parents. There are seventy inhabited planets, fifty suns,
thirty billion people, four hundred important storms, the
biggest at Latitude 473. The central government is on the
glorious planet, Cassidor VII—"

With a blank horror of what he was doing, Watcher
caught his roaring mind into a Dellian knot, and stopped
that devastating burst of revelation. He knew he would
never be caught like that again but—too late, he thought,
too late by far.

The woman wasn't quite so certain. She went out of
the room, and came back presently to where the middle-
aged Lieutenant Neslor was classifying her findings on
receptor spools.

The psychologist glanced up from her work and said
in an amazed voice, "Noble lady, his resistance during
the stoppage moment registered an equivalent of I.Q. 800.
Now, that's utterly impossible, particularly because he

started talking at a pressure point equivalent to I.Q. 167, which matches with his general appearance, and which you know, is average. There must be a system of mind training behind his resistance. And I think I found the clue in his reference to his Dellian ancestry. His graph squared in intensity when he used the word. This is very serious, and may cause great delay—unless we are prepared to break his mind."

The grand captain shook her head, said only, "Report further developments to me."

On the way to the transmitter, she paused to check the ship's position. A bleak smile touched her lips, as she saw on the reflector the shadow of a ship circling the brighter shadow of a sun. Marking time, she thought, and felt a chill of premonition. Was it possible that one man was going to hold up a ship strong enough to conquer an entire galaxy?

The senior ship meteorologist, Lieutenant Cannons, stood up from a chair as she came toward him across the vast floor of the transmission receiving room, where the Fifty Suns weather station still stood. He had graying hair, and he was very old, she remembered, very old. Walking toward him she thought: There was a slow pulse of life in these men who watched the great storms of space. There must be to them a sense of futility about it all, a timelessness. Storms that took a century or more to attain their full roaring maturity, such storms and the men who catalogued them must acquire a sort of affinity of spirit. The slow stateliness was in his voice, too, as he bowed with a measure of grace, and said, "Grand Captain, the Right Honorable Gloria Cecily, the Lady Laurr of Noble Laurr, I am honored by your personal presence."

She acknowledged the greeting, and then unwound the spool for him. He listened, frowning, then said: "The latitude he gave for the storm is a meaningless quantity. These incredible people have built up a sun relation system in the Greater Magellanic Cloud, in which the center is an arbitrary one having no recognizable connection with the magnetic center of the whole Cloud. Probably, they've picked some sun, called it center, and built their whole spatial geography around it."

The old man turned abruptly away from her, and led the way into the weather station, to the edge of the pit above which poised the reconstructed weather map.

"The map is utterly worthless to us," he said succinctly.

"What?"

She saw that he was staring at her, his china-blue eyes thoughtful. "Tell me, what is your idea of this map?"

The woman was silent, unwilling to commit herself in the face of so much definiteness. Then she frowned and said, "My impression is much as you described. They've got a system of their own here, and all we've got to do is find the key."

She continued more confidently, "Our main problems, it seems to me, would be to determine which direction we should go in the immediate vicinity of this weather station we've found. If we chose the wrong direction, there would be vexatious delay, and, throughout, our chief obstacle would be that we dare not go fast because of possible storms."

She looked at him questioningly as she ended and saw that he was shaking his head gravely.

"I'm afraid," he said, "it's not so simple as that. Those bright point-replicas of suns look the size of peas due to light distortion, but when examined through a metroscope they show only a few molecules in diameter. If that is their proportion to the suns they represent—"

She had learned in genuine crisis to hide her feelings from subordinates. She stood now, inwardly stunned, outwardly cool, thoughtful, calm. She said finally, "You mean each of those suns, their suns, is buried among about a thousand other suns?"

"Worse than that. I would say that they have only inhabited one system in ten thousand. We must never forget that the Greater Magellanic Cloud is a universe of over fifty million stars. That is a lot of sunshine." The old man concluded quietly, "If you wish, I will prepare orbits involving maximum speeds of ten light days a minute to all the nearest stars. We may strike it lucky."

The woman shook her head savagely. "One in ten thousand. Don't be foolish. I happen to know the law of averages that relates to ten thousand. We would have to visit a minimum of twenty-five hundred suns if we were lucky, thirty-five to fifty thousand if we were not. No, no—" a grim smile compressed her fine lips— "we are not going to spend five hundred years looking for a needle in a haystack. I'll trust to psychology before I'll trust to chance. We have the man who understands the map, and while it will take time, he will talk in the end."

She started to turn away, then stopped. "What," she asked, "about the building itself? Have you drawn any conclusions from its design?"

He nodded. "Of the type used in the galaxy about fifteen thousand years ago."

"Any improvements, changes?"

"None that I can see. One observer, who does all the work. Simple, primitive."

She stood thoughtful, shaking her head as if trying to clear away a mist. "It seems strange. Surely after fifteen thousand years they could have added something. Colonies are usually static, but not that static."

Three hours later, she was examining reports when her astro clanged twice, softly. Two messages—

The first was from Psychology House, a single question: "Have we permission to break the prisoner's mind?"

"No!" said Grand Captain Laurr.

The second question made her glance across at the orbit board. The board was aglitter with orbit symbols. That wretched old man, disobeying her injunction NOT to prepare any orbits. Smiling twistedly she walked over and studied the shining things, and finally sent an order to central engines. She watched as her great ship plunged into night. After all, she thought, there was such a thing as playing two games at the same time. Counterpoint was older in human relations than it was in music.

The first day she stared down at the outer planet of a blue-white sun. It floated in the darkness below the ship, an airless mass of rock and metal, drab and terrible as any meteorite, a world of primeval canyons and mountains untouched by the leavening breath of life. Spy rays showed only rock, endless rock, not a sign of movement or of past movement.

There were three other planets, one of them, a warm, green world where winds sighed through virgin forests and animals swarmed on the plains. Not a house showed, nor the erect form of a human being.

Grimly the woman said into the inter-ship communicator: "Exactly how far can our spy rays penetrate into the ground?"

"A hundred feet."

"Are there any metals which can simulate a hundred feet of earth?"

"Several, noble lady."

Dissatisfied, she broke the connection. There was no call that day from Psychology House.

The second day, a giant red sun swam into her impatient ken. Ninety-four planets swung in their great orbits around their massive parent. Two were habitable, but again there was the profusion of wilderness and of animals usually found only on planets untouched by the hand and metal of civilization.

The chief zoological officer reported the facts in his precise voice: "The percentage of animals parallels the mean for worlds not inhabited by intelligent beings."

The woman snapped: "Has it occurred to you that there may have been a deliberate policy to keep animal life abundant, and laws preventing the tilling of the soil even for pleasure?"

She did not expect, nor did she receive, an answer. And once more there was not a word from Lieutenant Nelsor, the chief psychologist.

The third sun was farther away. She had the speed stepped up to twenty light days a minute—and received a shocking reminder as the ship bludgeoned into a small storm. It must have been small because the shuddering of metal had barely begun, when it ended.

"There has been some talk," she said afterward to the thirty captains assembled in the captain's pool, "that we return to the galaxy and ask for an expedition that will uncover these hidden rascals. One of the more whining of the reports that have come to my ears suggests that, after all, we were on our way home when we made our discovery, and that our ten years in the Cloud have earned us a rest."

Her gray eyes flashed; her voice grew icy. "You may be sure that those who sponsor such defeatism are not the ones who would have to make the personal report of failure to his majesty's government. Therefore, let me assure the faint hearts and the homesick that we shall remain another ten years if it should prove necessary. Tell the officers and crew to act accordingly. That is all."

Back in the main bridge, she saw that there was still no call from Psychology House. There was a hot remnant of anger and impatience in her, as she dialed the number. But she controlled herself as the intent, intelligent face of Lieutenant Neslor appeared on the plate.

"What is happening, lieutenant?" she asked. "I am anxiously waiting for further information from the prisoner."

The woman psychologist shook her head. "Nothing to report."

"Nothing!" Her amazement was harsh in her voice.

"I have asked twice," was the answer, "for permission to break his mind. You must have known that I would not lightly suggest such a drastic step."

"Oh!" She had known, but the disapproval of the people at home, the necessity for accounting for any amoral action against individuals, had made refusal an automatic response. Now—Before she could speak, the psychologist continued:

"I have made some attempts to condition him in his sleep, stressing the uselessness of resisting Earth when eventual discovery is sure. But that has only convinced him that his earlier revelations were of no benefit to us."

The leader found her voice. "Do you really mean, lieutenant, that you have no plan other than violence? Nothing?"

In the astroplate, the image head made a negative movement. The psychologist said simply: "An 800 I.Q. resistance in a 167 I.Q. brain is something new in my experience."

The woman felt a great wonder. "I can't understand it," she complained. "I have a feeling we've missed some vital clue. Just like that, we run into a weather station in a system of fifty million suns, a station in which there is a human being who, contrary to all the laws of self-preservation, immediately kills himself to prevent himself from falling into our hands.

"The weather station itself is an old model galactic affair, which shows no improvements after fifteen thousand years; and yet the vastness of time elapsed, the caliber of the brains involved suggest that all the obvious changes should have been made.

"And the man's name, Watcher, is so typical of the ancient pre-spaceship method of calling names on Earth according to the trade. It is possible that even the sun, where he is watching, is a service heritage of his family. There's something—depressing—here somewhere that—"

She broke off, frowning: "What is your plan?" After a minute, she nodded. "I see . . . very well, bring him to one of the bedrooms in the main bridge. And forget that part about making up one of our strong-arm girls to look like me. I'll do everything that's necessary. Tomorrow. Fine."

Coldly she sat watching the prisoner's image on the plate. The man, Watcher, lay in bed, an almost motionless figure, eyes closed, but his face curiously tense. He looked, she thought, like someone discovering that for the first time in four days, the invisible force lines that had bound him had been withdrawn.

Beside her, the woman psychologist hissed: "He's still suspicious, and will probably remain so until you partially ease his mind. His general reactions will become more and more concentrated on one plan. Every minute that passes will increase his conviction that he will have only one chance to destroy the ship, and that he must be decisively ruthless regardless of risk. I have been conditioning him the past ten hours to resistance to us in a very subtle fashion. You will see in a moment . . . ah-h!"

Watcher was sitting up in bed. He poked a leg from under the sheets, then slid forward, and onto his feet. It was an oddly powerful movement. He stood for a moment, a tall figure in gray pajamas. He had evidently been planning his first actions because, after a swift look at the door, he walked over to a set of drawers built into one wall, tugged at them tentatively, and then jerked them open with an effortless strength, snapping their locks one by one.

Her own gasp was only an echo of the gasp of Lieutenant Neslor.

"Good heavens!" the psychologist said finally. "Don't ask me to explain how he's breaking those metal locks. Strength must be a by-product of his Dellian training. Noble lady—"

Her tone was anxious; and the grand captain looked at her. "Yes?"

"Do you think, under the circumstances, you should play such a personal role in his subjection? His strength is obviously such that he can break the body of anyone aboard—"

She was cut off by an imperious gesture. "I cannot," said the Right Honorable Gloria Cecily, "risk some fool making a mistake. I'll take an anti-pain pill. Tell me when it is time to go in."

Watcher felt cold, tense, as he entered the instrument room of the main bridge. He had found his clothes in some locked drawers. He hadn't known they were there, but the drawers aroused his curiosity. He made the preliminary Dellian extra energy movements; and the locks snapped before his superior strength.

Pausing on the threshold, he flicked his gaze through the great domed room. And after a moment his terrible fear that he and his kind were lost, suffered another transfusion of hope. He was actually free.

These people couldn't have the faintest suspicion of the truth. The great genius, Joseph M. Dell, must be a forgotten man on Earth. Their release of him must have behind it some plan of course but—

"Death," he thought ferociously, "death to them all, as they had once inflicted death, and would again."

He was examining the bank on bank of control boards when, out of the corner of his eyes, he saw the woman step from the nearby wall. He looked up, and thought with savage joy: The leader! They'd have guns protecting her, naturally, but they wouldn't know that all these days he had been frantically wondering how he could force the use of guns.

Surely to space, they *couldn't* be prepared to gather up his component elements again. Their very act of freeing him had showed psychological intentions.

Before he could speak, the woman said, smilingly: "I really shouldn't let you examine those controls. But we have decided on a different tactic with you. Freedom of the ship, an opportunity to meet the crew. We want to convince you . . . convince you—"

Something of the bleakness and implacableness of him must have touched her. She faltered, shook herself in transparent self-annoyance, then smiled more firmly, and went on in a persuasive tone: "We want you to realize that we're not ogres. We want you to end your alarm that we mean harm to your people. You must know, now that we have found you exist, that discovery is only a matter of time. Earth is not cruel, or dominating, at least not any more. The barest minimum of allegiance is demanded, and that only to the idea of a common unity, the indivisibility of space. It is required, too, that criminal laws be uniform, and that a high minimum wage for workers be maintained. In addition, wars of any kind are absolutely forbidden. Except for that, every planet or group of planets, can have its own form of government, trade with whom they please, live their own life. Surely, there is nothing terrible enough in all this to justify the curious attempt at suicide you made when we discovered the weather station."

He would, he thought, listening to her, break her head first. The best method would be to grab her by the feet, and smash her against the metal wall or floor. Bone would crush easily and the act would serve two vital purposes:

It would be a terrible and salutary warning to the other officers of the ship. And it would precipitate upon him the death fire of her guards. In these confines they would realize too late that only flame could stop him.

He took a step toward her. And began the faintly visible muscle and nerve movements so necessary to pumping the Dellian body to a pitch of superhuman capability.

The woman was saying: "You stated before that your people have inhabited fifty suns in this space. Why only fifty? In twelve thousand or more years, a population of twelve thousand billion would not be beyond possibility."

He took another step. And another. Then he knew that he must speak if he hoped to keep her unsuspicious for those vital seconds while he inched closer. Closer. He said, "About two thirds of our marriages are childless. It has been very unfortunate, but you see there are two types of us, and when intermarriage occurs as it does without hindrance—"

Almost he was near enough; he heard her say: "You mean a mutation has taken place; and the two don't mix?"

He didn't have to answer that. He was ten feet from her; and like a tiger he launched himself across the intervening gap.

The first fire beam ripped through his body too low to be fatal, but it brought a hot scalding nausea and a dreadful heaviness. He heard the grand captain scream: "Lieutenant Neslor, what are you doing?"

He had her then. His fingers were grabbing hard at her fending arm, when the second blow struck him high in the ribs and brought the blood frothing into his mouth. In spite of all his will, he felt his hands slipping from the woman. Oh space, how he would have liked to take her into the realm of death with him.

Once again the woman screamed: "Lieutenant Neslor, are you mad? *Cease fire!*"

Just before the third beam burned at him with indescribable violence, he thought with a final and tremendous sardonicism: "She still didn't suspect. But somebody did; somebody who at this ultimate moment had guessed the truth."

"Too late," he thought, "too late, you fools! Go ahead and hunt. They've had warning, time to conceal themselves even more thoroughly. And the Fifty Suns are scattered, scattered among a million stars, among—"

Death caught his thought.

The woman picked herself off the floor, and stood dizzily striving to draw her roughly handled senses back into her brain. She was vaguely aware of Lieutenant Neslor coming through a transmitter, pausing at the body of the Gisser Watcher then hurrying toward her.

"Are you all right, my dear? It was so hard firing through an astroplate that—"

"You mad woman!" the grand captain caught her breath. "Do you realize that a body can't be reconstituted once fire has destroyed vital organs. It is the one method that is final. We'll have to go home without—" She stopped. She saw that the psychologist was staring at her.

Lieutenant Neslor said, "His intention to attack was unmistakable and it was too soon according to my graphs. All the way through, he's never fitted anything in human psychology. At the very last possible moment I remembered Joseph Dell and the massacre of the Dellian supermen fifteen thousand years ago. Fantastic to think that some of them escaped and established a civilization in this remote part of space.

"Do you see now: Dellian—Joseph M. Dell—the inventor of the Dellian perfect robot."

Chapter One

THE street loud speaker clattered into life. A man's voice said resonantly:

"Attention, citizens of the planets of the Fifty Suns. This is the Earth battleship *Star Cluster*. In a few moments, the Right Honorable Gloria Cecily, Lady Laurr of Noble Laurr, Grand Captain of the *Star Cluster*, will make an announcement."

Maltby, who had been walking towards an airlift car, stopped as the voice sounded from the radio. He saw that other people were pausing also.

Lant was a new planet for him; its capitol city was delightfully rural after the densely populated Cassidor, where the Fifty Suns Space Navy had its main base. His own ship had landed the day before, on general orders commanding all warships to seek refuge immediately on the nearest inhabited planet.

It was an emergency order, with panic implicit in it. From what he had heard at officers' mess, it was clear that it had something to do with the Earth ship whose broadcast was now being transmitted over the general alarm system.

On the radio, the man's voice said impressively: "And here is Lady Laurr."

A young woman's clear, firm silvery voice began:

"People of the Fifty Suns, we *know* you are there.

"For several years, my ship the *Star Cluster*, has been mapping the Greater Magellanic Cloud. Accidentally, we ran into one of your space meteorological stations, and captured its attendant. Before he succeeded in killing himself, we learned that somewhere in this cloud of about

21

a hundred million stars, there are fifty inhabited sun systems with a total of seventy planets with human beings living on them.

"It is our intention to find you, though it may seem at first thought that it will be impossible for us to do so. Locating fifty suns scattered among a hundred million stars seems difficult in a purely mechanical way. But we have devised a solution to the problem that is only partly mechanical.

"Listen well now, people of the Fifty Suns. We know who you are. We know that you are the Dellian and non-Dellian robots—so called; not really robots at all, but flesh and blood humanoids. And, in looking through our history books, we have read about the foolish riots of fifteen thousand years ago that frightened you, and made you leave the main galaxy and seek sanctuary far away from human civilization.

"Fifteen thousand years is a long time. Men have changed. Such unpleasant incidents as your ancestors experienced are no longer possible. I say this to you in order to ease your fears. Because you must come back into the fold. You must join the Earth galactic union, subscribe to certain minimum regulations, and establish interstellar commercial ports.

"Because of your special reasons for concealing yourselves, you are allowed one sidereal week to reveal to us the location of your planets. During that time, we shall take no action. After that time, for each sidereal day that passes without contact being established, there will be a penalty.

"Of this you may be sure. We shall find you. And quickly!"

The speaker was silent, as if to let the meaning of the words sink in. Near Maltby, a man said: "Only one ship. What are we afraid of? Let's destroy it before it can go back to the galaxy and report our presence."

A woman said uneasily: "Is she telling the truth, or is she bluffing? Does she really believe they can locate us?"

A second man spoke gruffly: "It's impossible. It's the old needle in the haystack problem, only worse."

Maltby said nothing, but he was inclined to agree. It seemed to him that Grand Captain Laurr, of the Earth ship, was whistling in the greatest darkness that had ever hidden a civilization.

On the radio, the Right Honorable Gloria Cecily was speaking again:

"In the event that you do not keep time the way we do, a sidereal day is made up of twenty hours of a hundred minutes each. There are a hundred seconds in a minute, and in that second light travels 100,000 miles exactly. Our day is somewhat longer than the old style day in which a minute was sixty seconds, and light-speed 186,300-odd miles a second.

"Govern yourselves accordingly. One week from today I shall call again."

There was a pause. And then the voice of a man—not the one who had introduced the woman—said:

"Citizens of the Fifty Suns, that was a transcribed message. It was delivered about an hour ago, and was re-broadcast on the instructions of the Fifty Suns council in accordance with our desire to keep the populace abreast of all developments in this, the most serious danger that has ever threatened us.

"Continue about your daily business, and be assured that everything possible is being done. Further information will be given out as it is received.

"That is all for now."

Maltby climbed aboard the airlift car which settled down at his signal. As he sank into a vacant seat, a woman came over and sat down beside him. He felt the faintest tugging sensation at his mind. His eyes widened a little, but he gave no other sign that he had felt the probing of the woman spy's mind.

She said after a little: "Did you hear the broadcast?"

"Yes."

"What do you think of it?"

"The commander seemed very positive."

"Did you notice that she had identified all of us here in the Fifty Suns as Dellian and non-Dellian robots?"

He was not surprised that she had got it also. The

Earth people did not know that there was a third group in the Fifty Suns—the mixed men. For thousands of years after the migration, a Dellian and non-Dellian marriage had not produced children. Finally, by what was known as the cold-pressure system, children became possible. The result was the so-called Mixed Man, with two minds, Dellian physical strength and non-Dellian creative ability. The two minds, properly coordinated, could dominate any person who had only one mind.

Maltby was a Mixed Man. So was the woman sitting beside him, as he had recognized from the way she had momentarily stimulated his brain. The difference between them was, he had a legal status on Lant and other planets of the Fifty Suns. She didn't. If she were caught, she would be subject to imprisonment or death.

"We've been following you," she said, "intending to contact you, ever since our headquarters heard this message something over an hour ago. What do you think we should do?"

Maltby hesitated. It was hard for him to accept his role of hereditary leader of the Mixed Men; he who was also a captain in the Fifty Suns space fleet. Twenty years before, the Mixed Men had tried to seize control of the Fifty Suns. The attempt had ended in disastrous failure, as a result of which they were declared outlaws. Maltby, then a small boy, had been captured by a Dellian patrol party. The fleet educated him. He was an experiment. It was recognized that the problem of the Mixed Men would have to be solved. A prolonged effort was made to teach him loyalty to the Fifty Suns as a whole; and to a considerable extent it was a success. What his teachers didn't know was that they had in their power the nominal leader of the Mixed Men.

It had put a conflict into Maltby's mind, one which he had not yet resolved. He said slowly: "At the moment my feeling is that we should automatically stick with the group. Let us act openly with the Dellians and non-Dellians. After all, we too are of the Fifty Suns."

The woman said, "There has already been talk of the

possibility that we could gain some advantage by giving away the location of one of the planets."

For a moment, despite his own ambivalent training, that shocked Maltby. And yet, he could see what she meant. The situation was alive with dynamic potentialities. He thought ruefully: "I guess I'm not temperamentally suited for intrigue." He grew calmer, more thoughtful, more prepared to discuss the problem objectively: "If Earth located this civilization, and recognized its government, then no changes would be possible. Any plans we might have for altering the situation in our favor—"

The woman—she was a slim blonde—smiled grimly, a savage light in her blue eyes. "If we gave them away," she said, "we could make the condition that we would hereafter receive equal status. That's all we want, basically."

"Is it?" Maltby knew better, and he was not pleased. "I seem to remember the war we waged had other purposes."

"Well—" The woman was defiant—"who has a better right to the dominant position? We are physiologically superior to the Dellians and non-Dellians. For all we know, we may be the only super-race in the galaxy." She broke off tensely: "There's another, greater possibility: These Earth people have never run into Mixed Men. If we had the advantage of surprise—if we could get enough of our people aboard their ship—we might capture new, decisive weapons. Do you see?"

Maltby saw many things, including the fact that there was a great deal of wishful thinking involved. "My dear," he said, "we are a small group. Our revolution against the Fifty Suns government failed, despite initial surprise. It is possible that we might be able to do all these things, given time. But our ideas are bigger than our numbers."

"Hunston thinks the time to act is during a crisis."

"Hunston!" said Maltby involuntarily.

And then he was silent.

Alongside the colorful and demanding Hunston, Maltby felt himself drab. His was the unpopular role of holding in check the fierce passions of undisciplined young people. Through his followers, mostly elderly men, friends of his dead father, he could do nothing but advocate caution. It had proved a thankless task. Hunston was a sub-leader of the Mixed-Men. His dynamic program of action-now appealed to the younger people, to whom the disaster of the previous generation was mere hearsay. Their attitude was: "The leaders then made mistakes. We won't."

Maltby himself had no desire for dominance over the people of the Fifty Suns. For years, he had asked himself the question: "How can I direct the ambitions of the Mixed Men into less belligerent channels?" Up to now, he had found no ready solution. He said slowly, firmly: "When the group is threatened, the ranks must close. Whether we like it or not, we are of the Fifty Suns. It may be that it would be advisable to betray this civilization to Earth, but that is not something for us to decide an hour after the opportunity presents itself. Advise the hidden cities that I want three days of discussion and free criticism. On the fourth day there will be a plebiscite, on which the issue will be: betray or not betray? That is all."

From the corner of his eye, he saw that the woman was not pleased. Her face was suddenly sullen; there was suppressed anger in the way she held herself.

"My dear," he said gently, "surely you are not thinking in terms of going against the majority?"

He could see, then, from her changing expression, that he had started the old democratic conflicts in her mind. It was his great hold on all these people, the fact that the Mixed Men Council—of which he was head—appealed on all major issues directly to the group. Time had proved that plebiscites brought out the conservative instincts of a people. Individuals, who for months had talked angrily of the forthright steps that must be taken, grew cautious when confronted by a plebiscite ballot. Many a dangerous political storm had blown itself out in the ballot box.

The woman, who had been silent, said slowly: "In four days, some other group may have decided to do the betraying; and we will have lost the advantage. Hunston thinks that in a crisis government should act without delay. Later, it can ask the people if they think its action was correct."

For that at least Maltby had an adequate answer: "The fate of an entire civilization is involved. Shall one man or a small group commit, first, a few hundred thousand of their own people, and, through them, sixteen billion citizens of the Fifty Suns? I think not. But now, here is where I get off. Good luck."

He stood up, and presently climbed to the ground. He did not look back, as he headed for the steel barrier beyond which was one of several small bases which the Fifty Suns Military Forces maintained on the planet of Lant.

The guard at the gate examined his credentials with a frown, and then said in a formal tone: "Captain, I have orders to escort you to the Capitol building, where local government leaders are in conference with military commanders. Will you come peaceably?"

Outwardly, Maltby did not hesitate. "Of course," he said.

A minute later, he was in a military air car being flown back across the city.

It was not, as yet, he recognized, an inescapable situation. In an instant he could concentrate his two minds in a certain pattern, and control first his guard, and then the pilot of the craft.

He decided to do neither. It struck him that a conference of government leaders did not spell immediate danger for Captain Peter Maltby. Indeed, he could expect to learn something.

The small ship landed in a courtyard between two ivy-covered buildings. Maltby was taken through a door into a broad, brightly lighted corridor, and so was ushered into a room where a score of men sat around a conference table. His arrival had evidently been announced, for no one was talking as he entered. He glanced swiftly along the line of faces that turned towards him. Two he knew personally. Both wore the uniform of Commanding Officers of the fleet. Both nodded greeting. He acknowledged the recognition in each case with a nod of his own.

All the other men, including four men in uniform, he had not previously seen in person. He recognized several local government leaders, and several local officers. It was easy to distinguish the Dellian from the non-Dellian. The former were, without exception, fine, handsome, strong looking men. The latter varied widely. It was a pudgy non-Dellian at the head of the table facing the door, who stood up. Maltby recognized him from news photos as Andrew Craig, a local government minister. "Gentlemen," Craig began, "let us not be evasive with Captain Maltby."

He addressed himself to Maltby: "Captain, a number of conversations have been in progress in connection with the threat of the so-called Earth battleship, whose woman commander a short time ago made the announcement you probably heard."

Maltby inclined his head. "I heard it."

"Good. Here is the situation. It has already been more or less decided that we shall not reveal ourselves to this intruder, regardless of inducements offered. A few people argued that, now that Earth has come to the Greater Magellanic Cloud, discovery is inevitable sooner or later. But the time interval involved could be thousands of years. Our attitude is, let us stick together now, and refuse contact. During the next decade—and it will take that long—we can send expeditions to the main galaxy, and see just what is going on there. Having done that, we can then make our final decision on the matter of establishing relations. You can see that this is the sensible course."

He paused, and gazed expectantly at Maltby. There was in his manner a hint of anxiety. Maltby said in an even tone: "That is undoubtedly the sensible course."

An audible sigh of relief went up from several men.

"However," Maltby continued, "can you be sure that some group or planet will not reveal our location to the Earth ship? Many people, many planets, have individual interests."

"Of that," said the pudgy man, "we are well aware. Which is why you have been invited to this meeting."

Maltby wasn't sure that it had been precisely an invitation, but he made no comment.

The spokesman went on: "We have now received communications from all Fifty Sun governments. They are uniformly agreed that we must remain hidden. But all are equally aware that, unless we can obtain an agreement from the Mixed Men not to take advantage of this situation, then our unity will have been in vain."

For some minutes Maltby had guessed what was coming. And he had recognized it as a crisis in the relationship between Mixed Men and the people of the Fifty Suns. It was also, he saw clearly, a personal crisis for himself. He said: "Gentlemen, I have an idea that I am going to be asked to make contact with other Mixed Men. As a Captain in the Fifty Suns military arm, any such contact will place me immediately in a very difficult position."

Vice-admiral Dreehan, Commanding Officer of the Battleship *Atmion*, of which Maltby was assistant astrogator and chief meteorologist, spoke up: "Captain, you may agree freely to any proposal here made to you. Have no fear that your anomalous position is not appreciated."

"I should like," said Maltby, "to have that written into the minutes, and note taken."

Craig nodded at the stenographers. "Please note!" he said.

"Proceed," said Maltby.

"As you have guessed," Craig went on, "we want you to convey our proposals to the—" He paused, scowling a little, obviously reluctant to use a word that lent an aura of legitimacy to the outlaw group—"to the governing council of the Mixed Men. You have, we believe, opportunity to make such a contact."

"Years ago," acknowledged Maltby, "I informed my commanding officer that I had been approached by emissaries of the Mixed Men, and that permanent facilities for liaison existed on each planet of the Fifty Suns. It was decided at that time not to show any awareness of the existence of these agencies, as they would obviously go underground in a more thorough fashion—that is, they would not advise me of their future location."

Actually, the decision for him to inform the armed forces of the Fifty Suns that such agencies existed had been made by the plebiscite of the Mixed Men. It was felt that contact would be suspected, and therefore should be admitted. It was further believed that the Fifty Suns would not molest the agencies except in an emergency. The action had proved soundly based. But here was the emergency.

"Frankly," said the pudgy man, "it is our conviction that the Mixed Men are going to regard this situation as one which strengthens their bargaining position." He meant political blackmail, and it was a significant commentary of the situation that he did not say so. "I am empowered," Craig went on, "to offer limited citizenship rights, access to certain planets, eventual right to live in cities—with the whole problem of legal and political rights to be taken up every ten years, with assurance that each time—depending on behavior during the previous decade—further privileges will be granted."

He paused; and Maltby saw that everyone was looking at him with a kind of tense eagerness. A Dellian politician broke the silence: "What do you think of it?"

Maltby sighed. Before the arrival of the Earth ship, it would have been a remarkable offer. It was the old story of a concession made under pressure at a time when those who made it no longer controlled the situation. He said as much, not aggressively, but with a to-the-point candour. Even as he spoke, he thought over the terms, and it seemed to him that they were sound and honest. Knowing what he knew of the ambitions of certain groups among the Mixed Men, it seemed to him that further concessions would be as dangerous to them as to their peaceable neighbors. In view of the past, there had to be restrictions and a period of probation. Therefore, he tended to support the proposals, while recognizing that it would be hard, under the circumstances, to put them over. He made his point quietly; and finished: "We'll just have to wait and see."

There was a brief silence after he had spoken; and then a heavy-faced non-Dellian said harshly: "My own feeling is that we're wasting our time in this cowardly by-play. Although the Fifty Suns have been at peace for a long time, we still have more than a hundred battleships in service, not counting a host of smaller craft. Out there somewhere in space is one Earth battleship. I say, let's send the fleet to destroy it! That way we'll eliminate every human being who knows we exist. Ten thousand years may go by before they accidentally discover us again."

Vice-admiral Dreehan said: "We've discussed that. The reason it is inadvisable is very simple: The Earth people may have new weapons which could defeat us. We can't take the chance."

"I don't care what weapons one ship has," said the other flatly. "If the navy does its duty, all our problems will be solved by a single decisive action."

Craig said curtly: "That is a last resort." He faced Maltby again. "You may tell the Mixed Men that, if they turn down our offer, we do have a large fleet to use against the intruder. In other words, if they should pursue the course of betrayal, it would not necessarily gain them anything. You may go, Captain."

Chapter Two

ABOARD the Earth battleship, *Star Cluster*, Grand Captain, the Right Honorable Gloria Cecily, Lady Laurr of Noble Laurr, sat at her desk on the bridge, gazed out into space, and considered her situation.

In front of her was a multi-planal viewport, set at full transparency. Beyond was blackness with, here and there, stars. Magnification was at zero, and so only a few stars were visible, with occasional splotches of light to indicate the star density in that direction. The biggest and blurriest haze was to her left: The main galaxy, of which Earth was one planet of one system, one grain of sand in a cosmic desert.

The woman scarcely noticed. For years some variation of that fantastic scene had been part of her life. She saw it, and ignored it, in the same moment. She smiled now, a smile of decision; pressed a button. A man's face came on to the plate in front of her. She said without preamble: "I have been informed, Captain, that there is disgruntlement at our decision to remain in the Greater Magellanic Cloud and search for the Fifty Suns civilization."

The Captain hesitated, then said carefully: "Your excellency, I have heard that your determination to make this search does not meet with universal approval."

His changing of her phrase "our decision" to "your determination" did not escape her.

The man went on: "Naturally, I cannot speak for all the members of the crew, since there are thirty thousand of them."

"Naturally," she said. And there was irony in her tone.

The officer seemed not to hear. "It seems to me, your

excellency, that it might be a good idea to hold a general ballot on this matter."

"Nonsense. They'd all vote to go home. After ten years in space, they've become jellyfish. They have little mind and no purpose. Captain—" Her voice was soft, but there was a glint in her eyes—"I sense in your tone and bearing a sort of emotional agreement with this—this childish instinct of the group. Remember, the oldest law of space flight is that someone must have the will to go forward. Officers are selected with the utmost care because they must not give in to this blind desire to go home. It has been established that people who finally do rush madly to their planet, and their house, have a momentary emotional satisfaction, and then restlessly join up for another long voyage. We are too far from our galaxy to cater to such juvenile lack of discipline."

The officer said quietly: "I am familiar with these arguments."

"I am glad to hear it," said Grand Captain Laurr acidly. And broke the connection between them.

Next, she called Astrogation. A young officer answered. To him she said: "I want a series of orbits plotted that will take us through the Greater Magellanic Cloud in the quickest possible time. Before we're through, I want us to have been within five hundred light-years of every star in the system."

Some of the color faded from the youthful officer's face. "Your excellency," he gasped, "that is the most remarkable order that we have ever received. This cloud of stars is six thousand light-years in diameter. What velocity did you have in mind, remembering that we have no knowledge of the location of the storms here?"

The boy's reaction disconcerted her, in spite of herself. Just for an instant, she felt doubt. She had a brief abstract awareness of how great a volume of space she contemplated passing through.

The doubt passed. She stiffened herself. "I believe," she said, "that the density of storm areas in this system would limit us to about one light-year every thirty minutes."

She broke off curtly: "Have your chief advise me when these orbits have been completed."

"Yes, your excellency, said the young man. His voice was drab.

She broke that connection, sat back and manipulated a switch that altered the viewport in front of her into a reflecting surface. She stared at her image. She saw a slim, grim-faced, rather handsome young woman of thirty-five. The image was smiling faintly, ironically, an indication of her satisfaction with the two steps she had taken. The word would spread. People would begin to realize what she contemplated. There would be despair; then acceptance. She felt no regret. She had done what she had because she took it for granted that the governments of the Fifty Suns would not reveal the location of a single one of their planets.

She ate lunch alone on the bridge, feeling intense excitement. A struggle for control of the ship's destiny was imminent; and she knew that she must be prepared for every eventuality. Three calls came through before she had finished eating. She had set up an automatic busy signal; and so she ignored them. The busy signal meant: "I'm here, but don't bother me unless it's urgent." Each time the calls ceased within seconds.

After lunch, she lay down for a while to sleep and think. Presently, she rose, walked over to a matter transmitter, made the necessary adjustments—and stepped through to Psychology House half a mile away.

Lieutenant Neslor, the chief psychologist and a woman, emerged from a nearby room and greeted her warmly. The Grand Captain outlined her problems. The older woman nodded, and said:

"I thought you'd be down to see me. If you'll wait a moment, I'll turn my patient to an assistant; and then I'll talk to you."

By the time she returned, Lady Laurr had felt an incidental curiosity. "How many patients do you have here?"

The older woman's gray eyes studied her thoughtfully.

"My staff does about eight hundred hours of therapy a week."

"With your facilities, that sounds tremendous."

Lieutenant Neslor nodded. "It's been on the increase for several years."

Lady Gloria shrugged, and was about to dismiss the matter when another thought struck her. "What's the trouble?" she asked. "Homesickness?"

"I suppose you could call it that. We have several technical names for it." She broke off. "Now, don't you be too critical. This is a hard life for people whose work is purely routine. Big though the ship is, with each passing year its facilities are less satisfying to the individual."

The Right Honorable Gloria Cecily parted her lips to say that her own work was routine also. Just in time she realized that the remark would sound false, even condescending. Nevertheless, she shook her head impatiently. "I don't understand. We have everything aboard this ship. Equal numbers of men and women, endless activities, food in plenty and more entertainment than a person could desire in an entire lifetime. You can walk under growing trees beside ever-running streams. You can get married and divorced, though of course no children are allowed. There are gay bachelors aboard, and bachelor girls. Everyone has a room of his own, and the knowledge that his pay is accumulating, and that he can retire at the end of the voyage." She frowned. "And right now, with the discovery of this civilization of the Fifty Suns, the voyage should be very stimulating."

The older woman smiled. "Gloria, dear, you're not being very bright. It's stimulating to you and me because of our special positions. Personally, I'm looking forward to seeing how these people think and act. I've read up on the history of the so-called Dellian and non-Dellian robots, and there's a whole new world of discovery here —for me; but not for the man who cooks my meals."

The Grand Captain's face was determined again. "I'm afraid he'll just have to stick it out. And now, let's get to business. We've got a two-level problem: Keeping

control of the ship. Finding the Fifty Suns. In that order,
I think."

Their discussion lasted well into the main sleep period.
In the end Lady Laurr returned to the bridge, and to her
apartment, which adjoined it, conceived that both problems were, as she had suspected, predominantly psychological.

The week of grace went by uneventfully.

At the precise hour that it ended, the Grand Captain
called into council the divisional captains of her giant
ship. And with her first words struck at the heart of the
emotional tension she had divined was in the officers as
well as the men: "As I see it, ladies and gentlemen, we
must stay here until we find this civilization, even if it
means remaining for another ten years."

The captains looked at their neighbors, and stirred uneasily. There were thirty of them, all except four being
men.

The Right Honorable Gloria Cecily Laurr of Noble
Laurr went on: "Taking that into account, accepting the
fact that long-run strategies are in order, has anyone a
plan of procedure?"

Captain Wayless, chief of staff of the flight command,
said: "I am personally opposed to the notion that this
search should be continued."

The Grand Captain's eyes narrowed. She guessed from
the expressions of the others that Wayless was stating a
more generally held opinion than she had suspected. She
said as quietly as had he: "Captain, there are procedures
for overruling a ship's commanding officer. Why not
follow one of them?"

Captain Wayless was pale. "Very well, your excellency," he said. "I invoke clause 492 of the Regulations."

In spite of herself, his prompt acceptance of her chal-
lenge shocked her. She knew the clause, since it was a
limitation on her own power. No one could possibly
know all the regulations governing the minutiae of personnel control. But she had learned that each individual
knew the regulations relating to himself. When it came

to personal rights, everyone was a space-lawyer, herself included.

But she sat now, white-faced, as Captain Wayless read the clause in a resonant voice: "Limitation . . . circumstances justify the captains in council . . . a majority . . . two-thirds. . . . Original purpose of voyage . . ."

It was all there, as she recalled it, invoked against her now for the first time. The *Star Cluster* had been sent on a mapping expedition. The task was completed. In insisting on a change of purpose, she had brought her actions within the meaning of the regulation.

She waited till Wayless had put down the book. Then she said in a mild tone: "How do we vote?"

It was twenty-one against her, and five for her. Four officers abstained. Captain Dorothy Sturdevant, who headed the female clerical division, said, "Gloria, it had to be that way. We've been out a long time. Let someone else find this civilization."

The Grand Captain tapped with her pencil on the long, gleaming desk, an impatient gesture. But when she spoke, her voice was measured: "Regulation 492 gives me discretion to act as I see fit in a period varying between five and ten percent of the total length of the voyage to date, provided the discretionary power is not employed beyond six months. I therefore decree that we remain six months longer in the Greater Magellanic Cloud. And now, let us discuss ways and means of locating a planet of the Fifty Suns. Here are my ideas."

Coolly, she proceeded to give them.

Chapter Three

MALTBY was reading in his cabin aboard the Fifty Suns' battleship *Atmion* when the alarm sounded: "All personnel to stations!"

There was no whine of sirens, so it was not a battle alert. He put down his book, slipped into his coat, and headed for astrogation and instrument room. Several officers, including the ship's executive astrogational officer, were already there when he arrived. They nodded to him, rather curtly, but that was usual. He sat down at his desk, and took out of his pocket the tool of his trade: a slide rule with a radio attachment which connected with the nearest—in this case the ship's—mechanical brain.

He was in the act of taking out pencils and paper, when the ship moved under him. Simultaneously, a loud speaker came on; and the unmistakable voice of Commanding Officer Vice-admiral Dreehan said:

"This message is going to officers only. As you know, slightly more than a week ago, we were contacted by the Earth battleship *Star Cluster*, and given an ultimatum, the time limit for which expired five hours ago. Up till now, the various governments of our people have indicated that no further message has been forthcoming. Actually, a second ultimatum was received about three hours ago, but it contained an unexpected threat. It is believed that the public might be unduly alarmed if the nature of the threat was announced. The attitude of the governments will be that no second message was received. But here, for your private information, is the new ultimatum."

There was a pause, and then a deep, firm, resonant man's voice spoke: "Her excellency, the Right Honorable

Gloria Cecily, Lady Laurr of Noble Laurr, Grand Captain of the battleship *Star Cluster*, will now deliver her second message to the people of the Fifty Suns."

There was another pause. And then, instead of Grand Captain Laurr, Admiral Dreehan's voice came on again.

"I have been asked," he said, "to call your attention to this imposing list of titles. Apparently, a woman of so-called noble birth is in command of the enemy ship. That a woman should be commander seems very democratic, indicating equality of the sexes. But how did she gain her appointment? Through her rank? Besides, the very existence of rank is some indication of the kind of totalitarian government that exists in the main galaxy."

Maltby could not agree to the analysis. Titles were words that had meanings according to usage. In the Fifty Suns, there had been totalitarian eras where the leaders called themselves "Chief Servant." There had been "Presidents" whose whim could mean death for individuals, "Secretaries" who controlled governments absolutely, immensely dangerous individuals all, whose nominal rank covered a deadly reality. Furthermore, the desire for a verbal symbol of achievement permeated all human effort in every type of political system. Even as he spoke, "Admiral" Dreehan exercised his rank. In listening to this private transcription of an ultimatum "Captain" Maltby was being given a special privilege of rank and position. The "head" of a business, the "owner" of property, the trained "expert"—each in its fashion was rank. Each gave the possessor emotional satisfaction similar to that obtainable from position of any degree. In the Fifty Suns it had become popular to despise kings and dictators of all history. This attitude, in failing to take account of the circumstances, was as childish as its opposite: the inculcated worship of leaders. The Mixed Men, in their desperate situation, had reluctantly appointed an hereditary leader to avoid the bitter rivalry of ambitious men. Their plan had received a dangerous setback when the "heir" was captured. But the resulting struggle for power had decided them to reaffirm his status. It seemed to Maltby, ruefully, that no man had ever felt so little like an hereditary ruler. Yet even as he shifted uneasily under the rank, he recognized how necessary it had been. And how great was the obligation upon him to act decisively in a crisis. His thought ended, because her "excellency" was speaking.

Grand Captain the Right Honorable Gloria Cecily said:

"It is with regret that we who represent the Earth civilization recognize the recalcitrancy of the governments of the Fifty Suns. We can say in the most solemn fashion that the people have been misled. The coming of Earth power into the Greater Magellanic Cloud will be of benefit to all individuals and groups of all planets. Earth has much to offer. Earth guarantees to the individual basic rights under law, guarantees to the group basic freedoms and economic prosperity, and requires all government to be elective by secret ballot.

"Earth does not permit a separate sovereign state *anywhere in the universe.*

"Such a separate military power could strike at the heart of the human-controlled galaxy, and drop bombs on densely populated planets. That has happened. You may guess what we did to the governments who sponsored such a project. You cannot escape us. If by any chance we should fail now with our one ship to locate you, then within a few years ten thousand ships will be here searching. This is one thing we never delay on. From our point of view, it is safer to destroy an entire civilization than let it exist as a cancer in the greater culture from which it sprang.

"However, we do not think that we shall fail. Starting now, my great battleship, *Star Culture,* will cruise on a definite course through the Greater Magellanic Cloud. It will take us several years to pass within five hundred light years of every sun in the system. As we move along, we shall direct cosmic-ray bombs at random towards the planets of most of the stars in any given area of space.

"Realizing that such a threat might make you afraid to trust yourselves to us, I have indicated why we adopt this admittedly merciless attitude. It is not yet too late to reveal yourselves. At any moment the government of any planet can broadcast its willingness to identify the location of the Fifty Suns. The first planet to do so will henceforth, and for all future time, be the capital of the Fifty Suns. The first individual or group who gives us a clue to the location of his or its planet will receive a gift of one billion platinum dollars, good anywhere in the main galaxy, or if you prefer, the equivalent sum in your own money.

"Have no fear. My ship can protect you against the organized might of the Fifty Suns military forces. And now, as an evidence of our determination, I shall have our chief astrogator broadcast the figures that will enable you to follow our course through the Cloud."

The message ended abruptly. Admiral Dreehan came on and said: "I shall presently give these figures to the Astrogation department, since it is our intention to follow the *Star Cluster*, and observe the result of its announced program. However, I have been asked to call your attention to another implication to the broadcast which Lady Laurr has made to us. Her manner, tone and wording suggest that she commands a very big ship." The Admiral went on quickly: "Please do not imagine that we are jumping to any conclusions, but consider some of her statements. She says that the *Star Cluster* will "direct" cosmic-ray bombs to most of the planets of the Cloud. Suppose when reduced to common sense she meant one bomb for every hundred planets. That would still require several million bombs. But our own bomb factories can turn out only one cosmic-ray unit every four days. At a minimum, such a factory would need a square mile of floor space. Then, again, she stated that her one ship can protect traitors against the Fifty Suns military forces. At the moment we have more than a hundred battleships in service in addition to four hundred cruisers and thousands of smaller craft. Let's consider also the original purpose of the *Star Cluster* in the Greater Magellanic Cloud. It was, by their own admission, a star mapping expedition. Our own mapping ships are small obsolete models. It seems hard to believe that Earth would assign one of their greatest and most powerful ships to so routine a task." The Admiral broke off. "I should like all officers to prepare for me their reactions to the foregoing statements. And now, that's all for most of you. I shall broadcast for Astrogation and Meteorology the figures supplied us by the *Star Cluster*."

It required just over five hours of sustained, careful work to orient the map furnished by the *Star Cluster* to the long-established star map system of the Fifty Suns. At that time it was estimated that the *Atmion* was about 1400 light years away from the Earth ship.

The distance was unimportant. They knew the location of all storms in the Greater Magellanic Cloud. And so they easily plotted an orbit that permitted a velocity of approximately half a light-year a minute.

The prolonged effort tired Maltby. As soon as his share of the task was finished, he retreated to his cabin, and slept.

He woke to the sound of an alarm bell ringing. Quickly, he switched on a viewplate that connected with the bridge. The fact that a picture came on immediately indicated that officers were being permitted to watch events. He saw on the plate that it was focussed at full magnification on a distant point of light. The light moved, and the plate kept adjusting, trying to hold it near center.

A voice said: "According to our automatic calculators, the *Star Cluster* is now approximately a third of a light year away."

Maltby frowned at the explanation, because it was not properly worded. The speaker meant that the two vessels were within each other's upper-reconance fields, a secondary phenomenon of sub-space radio, and a kind of damped echo of the virtually unlimited lower-resonance range. It was impossible to tell how far away the Earth ship was, except that it could not be farther than a third of a light year. It might be only a few hundred miles, though that was doubtful. There were radar devices for short-distance detection of objects in space.

The voice went on: "We have reduced our own speed to ten light-days a minute. Since we are following the course broadcast by the Earth ship, and have not lost her, we can assume that we are matching her velocity."

That statement, also was not exact. It was possible to approximate, but impossible to *match* velocities with a ship traveling at more than light-speed. The error would show up as soon as the two ships lost touch with each other's upper-resonance fields. Even as he had the thought, the light on the plate winked out.

Maltby waited, and finally the announcer said unhappily: "Please do not be alarmed. I have been told contact will probably be re-established."

An hour went by, and the light did not reappear. Maltby had long since ceased paying more than sporadic attention to the viewplate. His mind was on what Admiral Drechan had said about the size of the *Star Cluster*.

He realized the commanding officer had stated the situation fairly. It was a problem laden with dangerous possibilities. It seemed impossible that any vessel could be as big as Grand Captain Laurr had implied. And therefore the Earth ship was putting on a bluff. At least a part of the proof would be in the number of bombs she set off.

On six successive days the *Atmion* entered the upper resonance field of the Earth ship. Each time she maintained contact as long as possible; and then, having verified the enemy vessel's route, examined the planets of nearby suns. Only once did they find evidence of destruction. And the bomb must have been badly aimed, for it had hit an outer planet normally too cold and remote for its sun to support life.

It was not cold now, but a seething hell of nuclear energy that had fired the rocky crust and penetrated to the metallic core itself. A miniature sun blazed there. The sight of it alarmed no one aboard the *Atmion*. The probability that one of a hundred bombs would strike an inhabited planet was mathematically so close to zero that the difference didn't count.

It was on the sixth day of the search when Maltby's viewplate clicked on; and the image of Vice-admiral Dreehan's face appeared on it. "Captain Maltby, will you report to my office?"

"Yes, sir."

Maltby went at once. The adjutant in charge nodded recognition, and admitted him to Dreehan's cabin. Maltby found the commanding officer sitting in a chair, contemplating what looked like a radiogram. The older man laid the document face down, and motioned Maltby to sit down in the chair across the desk.

"Captain, what is your status among the Mixed Men?"

So they had finally got around to that basic question. Maltby did not feel alarmed. He stared at the officer, and allowed an expression of puzzlement to creep over his face. Dreehan was a middle-aged Dellian with the fine physique and handsome appearance of his kind. Maltby said: "I couldn't tell you exactly how they regard me. Partly as a traitor, I think. Whenever they contact me—which I always report to my superiors—I urge the agent who talks to me to tell his superiors that I recommend a policy of conciliation and integrity."

Dreehan seemed to consider that, and then he said: "What do the Mixed Men think of this business?"

"I'm not sure. My contact is too vague."

"Still, you probably have some idea."

"As I understand it," said Maltby, "a minority group among them believes that Earth will locate the Fifty Suns, sooner or later, so—they argue—advantage should be taken of the present position. The majority, which is tired of living in hiding, has definitely voted to go along with the rest of the Fifty Suns."

"By what percentage?"

"Just over four to one." Maltby spoke the lie without hesitation.

Dreehan hesitated; then, "Is there any possibility that the dissident minority will act unilaterally?"

Maltby said quickly: "They might want to, but they can't—so I've been assured."

"Why can't they?"

"They do not have a really skillful space meteorologist among them."

That was also a lie. The problem went deeper than any skill possessed by either group. The fact was that Hunston wanted to gain control of the Mixed Men by legal means. So long as he believed that he could do so, he would not take the law into his own hands—so Maltby's advisers had informed him. On that information, he now based his verbal web of falsehood and truth.

Dreehan seemed to be considering his words. He said finally: "The governments of the Fifty Suns are alarmed by the nature of the latest ultimatum—which you have heard—in that it offers such an ideal opportunity to the Mixed Men. They can betray us, and gain advantages as great as might have been theirs had they won the war a generation ago."

There was nothing Maltby could say to that except repeat a variation of his earler lie: "I think the four to one victory of those who prefer to stick with the Fifty Suns shows the trend."

Once more there was a pause. And Maltby wondered what was really behind the interview. Surely they couldn't be basing their hopes on reassurances from Captain Peter Maltby. Dreehan cleared his throat: "Captain, I've heard a great deal about the so-called double mind of the Mixed Men, without ever getting a clear explanation of how it works and what it does. Will you enlighten me?"

"It's really quite unimportant." Maltby spoke his third lie quietly. "I think the fear of it during the war had a great deal to do with the ferocity with which the final battles were fought. You know what a normal brain is like—innumerable cells, each one separately connectable to those adjoining it. On that level, the brain of the Mixed Man is no different than yours. Go down another level, and you have in each cell of a Mixed Man a whole series of large, protein, *paired* molecules. Yours are not paired; his are."

"But what does that do?"

The Mixed Man has the Dellian ability to resist the breaking down of his mind, and the non-Dellian potentiality for creative work."

"That's all?"

"That's all that I know of, sir," lied Maltby.

"What about that devastating hypnosis they were supposed to have? There is no clear record of how that worked."

Maltby said, "I understand they used hypnotic *devices*, a very different thing. It caused a confused terror of the unknown."

Dreehan seemed to come to a decision. He picked up the radiogram, and handed it to Maltby. "This came for you," he said. He added frankly: "If it's in code, we haven't been able to break it."

It was in code all right. Maltby saw that in the first glance. And this was what the Admiral had been leading up to.

The message read:

TO: Captain Peter Maltby,
      Aboard battleship *Atmion*

The government of the Mixed Men wishes to thank you for acting as mediator in the negotiations with the governments of the Fifty Suns. Please be assured that agreements will be lived up to fully, and that the Mixed Men as a group are anxious to obtain the privileges which have been offered.

There was no signature. Which meant that the call for help had been sent by sub-space radio, and monitored directly by the *Atmion*.

He had to pretend of course that he didn't know that—until he could make up his mind what to do. He said in a puzzled tone: "I notice there's no signature. Was that left off on purpose?"

Vice-admiral Dreehan looked disappointed. "Your guess is as good as mine."

Maltby felt briefly sorry for the officer. No Dellian or non-Dellian would ever break the code of that message. Solving the secret of it depended on having two minds trained to associate. The training was so basic in the education of Mixed Men that Maltby had received a full quota before he was captured more than twenty years before.

The essential meat of the real message was that the minority group had announced its intention of contacting the *Star Cluster*, and had begun a week-long campaign to gain support for the action. Their platform warned that only those who supported them would benefit from the betrayal.

He would have to go there in person. How? His eyes widened a little as he realized that he had only one available method of transportation: this ship. Abruptly, he knew that he had to do it. He began to tense his muscles in the Dellian fashion. He could feel the electric excitement of that stimulation. All in a moment his minds were strong enough.

He sensed the near presence of another mind. He waited till the sensation seemed to be a part of his own body, then he thought: "Blankness!" For a moment he held conscious thought away from his own brain. Finally, he stood up. Vice admiral Dreehan stood up also in exactly the same way, with the same movements, as if his muscles were controlled by Maltby's brain. Which they were. He walked to the instrument board, touched a switch. "Give me the engine room," he said.

With Maltby's mind directing his voice and his actions, he gave the orders that set the *Atmion* on a course that would bring it presently to the hidden capital city of the Mixed Men.

Chapter Four

GRAND CAPTAIN LAURR read the notice of "Nulli-fication," sat for a few minutes with fists clenched, in anger. And then controlling herself, called Captain Way-less. The officer's face stiffened as he saw who it was. "Captain," she said plaintively, "I have just read your document with its twenty-four signatures."

"It's legal, I believe," he said in a formal tone.

"Oh, I'm very sure of that," she retorted. She caught herself, and went on: "Captain, why this desperate de-termination to go home immediately? Life is more than legality. We're engaged in a great adventure. Surely you have some of that feeling left in you."

"Madam," was the cool reply, "I have both admiration and affection for you. You have tremendous administra-tive ability, but you do tend to project your own ideas, and are amazed and hurt when other people have notions different from your own. You are right so often that you lose sight of the fact that once in a while you may be wrong. That is why a big ship like this has thirty captains to advise you, and, in an emergency, or actually at any time, overrule you according to prescribed regulations. Believe me, we all love you. But we know our duty to the rest of those aboard."

"But you're wrong. We can force this civilization out into the open." She hesitated, then: "Captain, won't you please go along with me just this once?"

It was a personal appeal, and she regretted almost im-mediately that she had made it. The request seemed to release his tension. He laughed, tried to hold himself, then laughed again.

"Madam, I beg your pardon," he said finally. "Please forgive me."

She was stiff. "What amused you?"

He was sober-faced again. "The phrase 'Just this once.' Lady Laurr, have you no recollection of ever having asked us to support some plan of yours before?"

"Perhaps a couple of times." She spoke with abrupt caution, remembering.

"I haven't figured it out," said Captain Wayless, "But just on a rough estimate I would say that you have either asked for our support on a personal basis or else have used your legal command-status no less than a hundred times on this voyage to put over or enforce some idea of your own. Now, for once, the legality is being used against you. And you resent it bitterly."

"I'm not bitter. I'm—" She broke off. "Ohhhhh, I can see there's no use talking to you. For some reason or other you've decided that six months is all eternity."

"It's not a matter of the time. It's a matter of the purpose. You believe without evidence that you can find fifty suns scattered among a hundred million. A big ship just does not take a one-in-two million chance of that kind. If you can't see that, then for once we have to overrule you, regardless of our personal affection for you."

The Grand Captain hesitated. The argument was going against her. She saw the need for a more careful presentation of her reasons. She said slowly: "Captain, this is not a mechanical problem. If we were depending on chance alone, then your attitude would be correct. Our hope must be based on psychology."

Captain Wayless said quietly: "Those of us who signed the 'Nullification' did not do so lightly. We discussed the psychological aspect."

"And on what did you base your rejection of it? Ignorance?"

It was a sharp remark, and she saw that he was irritated. He said formally: "Madam, we have on occasion noted with misgivings your tendency to rely almost exclusively on the advice offered you by Lieutenant Neslor. These meetings you have with her are always private. What is said in them is never brought into the open, except that suddenly you make a move based on what she has told you."

The picture startled her a little. She said defensively: "I confess I hadn't thought of it that way. I merely went to the legally appointed chief psychologist aboard this ship."

Captain Wayless went on: "If Lieutenant Neslor's advice is so valuable, then she should be raised to Captain's rank, and permitted to air her views before the other captains." He shrugged; and he must almost have read her thought. Because, before she could utter the words, he said: "And please don't say that you will immediately make the appointment. It takes a month for such a promotion to be put through even if no one objects; and the new captain then sits silent for two months learning the procedure at a council meeting."

Lady Laurr said grimly: "You won't permit such a three months delay?"

"No."

"You won't consider by-passing ordinary procedure in making such an appointment?"

"In an emergency, yes. But this is merely a notion of yours for finding a lost civilization—which will be searched for, and found eventually, by an expedition dispatched for that puropse."

"Then you insist on 'Nullification'?"

"Yes."

"Very well. I shall order a plebiscite for two weeks from today. If it goes against me, and if nothing else turns up, we start for home."

With a gesture, she broke the connection.

She thought of herself consciously as engaged in warfare on two levels. On the one level, there was the struggle against Captain Wayless, and the four-fifth majority that had enabled him to force a plebiscite. On the other there was the fight she was waging to force the Fifty Suns people out into the open. On both levels, she had just begun to fight. She called "Communication." Captain Gorson answered. She said: "Are we still in touch with the Fifty Suns ship that is observing us?"

"No. I reported to you when we lost contact. It has not yet been established." He volunteered: "They'll probably pick us up again tomorrow when we broadcast our position at that time."

"Advise me."

"Of course."

She broke that connection, and called "Weapons." A subordinate answered, but she waited patiently till the Captain in charge was called. Then:

"How many bombs have you dropped?"

"Seven altogether."

"All dropped random?"

"It's the simplest method, Madam. Probability protects us from hitting a planet capable of supporting life."

She nodded, but sat frowning anxiously. She said, finally, feeling the need to re-state the situation: "Intellectually, I agree with that. Emotionally—" She broke off. "A single mistake, Captain, and you and I would be put on trial for our lives if it were ever found out."

He was grim. "I am familiar with that law, your excellency. It is one of the hazards of being in charge of 'Weapons.' " He hesitated, then: "My feeling is that you made a very dangerous threat—dangerous to us, that is. People should not be subjected to such pressures."

She said curtly: "That's my responsibility!" And broke the connection.

She stood up then, and paced the floor. Two weeks! It seemed impossible that anything could happen before then. In two weeks, as she had planned it, the psychological pressure on the Dellians and non-Dellians would barely have begun.

Thought of them reminded her. She walked swiftly to the matter transmitter, made the adjustments—and stepped through to the centrally located library, just over a third of a mile from her quarters.

She found herself in the private office of the chief librarian, who was sitting at her desk, writing. The Grand

Captain began instantly: "Jane, have you got that information on the Dellian riots of—"

The librarian started, half-rose from her chair, then sat down again. She sighed. "Gloria, you'll be the death of me. Can't you even say hello before you start in?"

The Grand Captain felt contrite. "I'm sorry. I was intent. But have you—"

"Yes, I have. If you'd waited another ten minutes, it would have been sent up to you in an orderly fashion. Have you had dinner yet?"

"Dinner! No, of course not."

"I love the way you say that. And, knowing you, I know exactly what you mean. Well, you're coming to dinner with me. And there'll be no discussion of Dellians or non-Dellians until after we've eaten."

"It's impossible, Jane. I just can't give the time right now—"

The older woman had climbed to her feet. Now, she came around the desk, and took Lady Laurr firmly by the arm. "Oh, you can't. Then just consider this. You will not receive any information from me until you've had dinner. And go right ahead and invoke your laws and regulations, and see if I care. Come along now."

For a second she resisted. Then she thought wearily: "It's this damned human factor. It's too hard to make people realize!" That tension ended also, and she had a sudden picture of herself, grim and intent, as if the fate of the universe rested on her shoulders. Slowly, she relaxed. She said: "Thank you, Jane. I'd love to have a glass of wine and some dinner."

But she did not forget that she was right; that, though she might relax for an hour, the reality remained. The Fifty Suns had to be found now for a reason that was only gradually maturing in her brain in all its deadly potentialities.

After dinner, with soft music playing in the background, they discussed the Fifty Suns civilization. The historical outline, as given by the librarian, was remarkably simple and straightforward.

Some fifteen thousand years before, Joseph M. Dell had

developed an early variation of the matter transmitter. The machine required mechanical synthesis of certain types of tissue, particularly of the endocrine glands, that could not be properly scanned. Since a human being could step in at one end, and emerge an instant later a thousand miles or more—or less—away, it was not immediately noticed that extremely subtle changes were taking place in the individuals who used the method of teleportation.

It was not that anything was missing, though Dellians were always afterward slow at creative work. But in some respects something seemed to have been added.

The Dellian proved to be less subject to nervous strain. His physical strength far exceeded anything ever dreamed of by human beings. He could build himself up to super-human effort by a curious process of internal stepping up of muscular tension.

Naturally—the librarian was ironic when she came to that part—they were called robots by the more alarmed of human beings. The name did not disturb the Dellians, but it excited humans to a height of hatred that was not immediately suspected by the authorities.

There was a period when mobs raged along the streets lynching Dellians. Human friends of the Dellians persuaded the government to let them migrate. Until now, no one had ever known where they had gone to.

The Right Honorable Gloria Cecily sat thoughtful for a while after the account was completed. She said finally: "You haven't been really helpful. I knew all that, except for a couple of minor details."

She was aware of the older woman studying her with shrewd blue eyes. "Gloria, what are you after? When you talk like that, you're usually trying to prove a theory of your own."

The remark hit home. The Grand Captain saw that it might be dangerous for her to admit such a thing. People who tried to force facts to fit their own private theories were unscientific. She had frequently been very sharp with officers who uttered vague opinions. She said slowly: "I simply want all the information we can get. It's obvious that when a mutation like the Dellian is off somewhere for a hundred and fifty centuries all the possible eventualities will have taken place. My attitude is, we can't afford to miss a single point that is available."

The librarian nodded. Watching her, Lady Laurr decided that the explanation had proved satisfactory; and that the momentary insight had faded from the forefront of the other's mind.

She stood up. She couldn't take the chance of any further revelations. The second one might not be so easy to dismiss. She said good night casually, and returned to her quarters. After a few minutes of thought, she called "Biology," and asked as her first question: "Doctor, I have previously sent you information on the Dellian and non-Dellian peoples of the Fifty Suns. In your opinion, would it be possible for a Dellian and non-Dellian—married to each other—to have children?"

The biologist was a slow-thinking man, who drawled when he spoke. "History says no," he said.

"What do you say?"

"I could do it."

"That," said Grand Captain Laurr triumphantly, "is what I wanted to hear."

The stimulation the information brought her did not fade until she crept into bed hours later. She turned out the light, then, and lay for a while staring out into space.

The great night was slightly changed. The points of light were differently arranged, but, without magnification, she had no visual evidence that she was actually in the Greater Magellanic Cloud. Not more than a hundred individual stars showed as separate units. Here and there was a fuzziness of light that indicated the presence of hundreds of thousands of stars, perhaps millions.

On impulse, she reached toward the vision control, and turned the magnification to full.

Splendor.

A billion stars blazed at her. She saw the near brilliance of innumerable stars in the Cloud, and the vast spiral wheel of the main galaxy, impregnated now with more light-points than could ever be counted. And all that she could see was a mere speck in the cosmic scheme of things. Where had it come from? Tens of thousands of generations of human beings had lived and died, and there was still not even the beginning of a satisfactory answer.

She reduced magnification to zero, and brought the universe back to the level of her own senses. Wide-eyed, she thought: "Suppose they did produce a cross-breed of the Dellian and non-Dellian? How could that affect me in two weeks?"

She couldn't imagine. She slept restlessly.

Morning . . . As she ate her lean breakfast, it struck her that only thirteen days remained. The impact of that hit her suddenly. She got up from the table, gloomily conscious that she was living in a dream world. Unless she took positive action, the entire enterprise upon which she had launched the great ship would collapse. She headed decisively for the control bridge, and called Communication. "Captain," she said to the officer who answered, "are we in upper resonance contact with the Fifty Suns' ship that is trailing us?"

"No, madam."

That was disappointing. Now that she had made up her mind, any delay was irritating. She hesitated, finally sighed her acceptance of the reality, and said, "The moment contact is made, communicate to Weapons."

"Very well, madam."

She broke connection, and called Weapons. The proud-faced officer commanding that department swallowed as she explained her purpose. He protested finally, "But, madam, this would reveal our greatest weapon. Suppose—"

"Suppose nothing!" Her fury was instant. "At this stage we have nothing to lose. We have failed to lure the Fifty Suns fleet. I order you to capture that one vessel. All the Navigation officers aboard will probably be ordered to commit suicide, but we'll get around that."

The officer frowned thoughtfully, then nodded. "The danger is that someone outside the field will detect it, and analyze it. But if you feel we should take that risk—"

The Right Honorable Gloria turned presently to other tasks, but a part of her mind never quite let go of the command she had given. She grew restless finally when no further call came, and again contacted Communication. But there was nothing. The Fifty Suns ship was not in range.

A day went by, then another. And still no contact.

By the fourth day, the Grand Captain of the *Star Cluster* was a very difficult person to get along with. And that day also went by without incident.

Chapter Five

"PLANET below!" said Vice-admiral Dreehan.

Maltby, who had been cat-napping, woke with a start, climbed to his feet, and went to the controls.

Under his direction, the ship moved rapidly from ten thousand miles above the surface to a thousand, and then to less than a hundred miles. Through magnification, he examined the terrain; and presently, though he had never seen it before, his memory brought up photographic maps he had been shown in the past.

Rapidly, now, the *Atmion* headed towards the largest of the cave entrances that led down to the hidden capitol of the Mixed Men. As a final precaution, he checked once more to make sure that junior officers were not able to watch what was happening in their viewplates—all fourteen senior key men were under his control—and then boldly he nosed the ship into the opening.

He watched tensely. He had radioed the leaders who supported him that he was coming. They had called back to say that all would be in readiness. But it was possible for a slip-up to occur. And here at the entrance a ship would be at the mercy of ground defenses.

The darkness of the cave closed around them. He sat with fingers on the searchlight switch, watching the night ahead. Suddenly, a light flickered far below. Maltby waited to make sure that it would not go out and then flicked the switch.

Instantly, the searchlights glared, lighting up the cave from ceiling to floor and into the distance ahead. The ship cruised forward, and gradually downward. An hour went by; and still there was no indication that the end of the journey was near.

The cave curved and twisted, downward and sideways and upwards. Several times he had the feeling that they were going back the way they had come. He could have kept track on an automatic graph, but he had been asked even before the *Atmion* neared the planet not to do so. It was said that no living person knew exactly where under the planet's crust the capitol was located. Other Mixed Men cities on still other planets were hidden in the same way.

Twelve hours passed. Twice Maltby had turned the control over to the vice-admiral while he slept. Now, he was in charge while the officer dozed peacefully on the cot in the corner.

Thirty hours! Physically worn out, and amazed, Maltby wakened Dreehan, and lay down. He had scarcely closed his eyes when the officer said:

"Buildings ahead, captain. Lights."

Maltby made a leap for the controls; and a few minutes later was guiding the ship over a city of about eighty thousand population. He had been told that no vessel of its size had ever been in the caves; and therefore at this moment it would be the object of attention by all individuals and groups. He switched on ordinary radio and turned the dial till he heard a voice. He heard: ". . . and Peter Maltby, our hereditary leader, has temporarily taken over the battleship *Atmion*, in order that he might personally reason with those who—"

Maltby clicked it off. The people were learning that he was here. In the plate, he searched the city below for Hunston's headquarters. He recognized the building from the description he had been radioed, and stopped the *Atmion* directly over it.

He focussed an energy screen on the center of the street a block away. Then, swiftly, he laid down other screens till the area was completely blocked off. People could enter the screen area without noticing that they were coming into a trap, but they could not leave it. Invisible from the outside, the screen had a purplish tint when seen from inside. It gave anyone who touched it from the inner section a powerful electric shock.

Since Hunston lived at his headquarters, it seemed likely that he was now unable to escape. Maltby did not delude himself that the action would be decisive. This was a struggle for political control, which might be influenced by force, but would not be resolved on that basis alone. In that struggle, his very method of arrival had given his enemies a powerful argument against him. "Look," they would undoubtedly say, "one Mixed Man was able to take over a battleship—proof of our superiority." That was heady stuff for people whose ambition had been starved for a quarter of a century.

In the viewplate he saw that small craft were approaching. He contacted them by radio, identified those aboard as leaders who supported him, and presently watched as his officer-controls personally admitted them to the airlock. Minutes later he was shaking hands with men he had never before seen in person.

Tactical and strategical discussions began almost immediately. Several men who came aboard felt that Hunston should be executed. A majority believed that he should be imprisoned. Maltby listened uneasily to both groups, conscious that in a sense the men on the scene were the best judges. On the other hand, their very closeness to the danger had made them tense. It was even possible that he, who had watched this scene from afar, might have a more detached, and, therefore, sounder attitude. That was a guess only, and he did not give too much weight to it. Nevertheless, he had begun to regard himself as being in the role of an arbiter when, abruptly, both groups began to question him.

"Can we be sure that the Fifty Suns will remain firm in their refusal to establish contact with the Earth ship?"

"Was there any sign of weakening from what you saw and heard?"

"Why was the second ultimatum withheld from the people?"

"Is the battleship *Atmion* the only ship assigned to follow the *Star Cluster?*"

"Is there perhaps some secret purpose behind such a following move?"

"What would our position be if, suddenly, the Fifty Suns surrendered their location?"

For a little while, Maltby felt overwhelmed. And then, as he saw that the questions followed a pattern, and that behind them was a false implication, he held up his hand and said: "Gentlemen, you seem to be laboring under the theory that, if the other governments should change their minds, we might still rush in and gain an advantage. This is not so. Our position is that we stand solidly with the Fifty Suns whatever their decision. We act as one with the group. We do not maneuver for special advantage other than within the frame of the offer that has been made to us." He finished in a more personal, less severe tone: "I can see you have all been under immense pressure. Believe me, I appreciate your position, as a group and as individuals. But we've got to maintain our integrity. We cannot be opportunistic in this crisis."

The men looked at each other. Some, particularly the younger men, seemed unhappy, as if they were being asked to swallow a bitter pill. But in the end they all agreed to support the plan for the time being.

Then came the crucial question: "What about Hunston?"

Maltby said coolly: "I'd like to talk to him."

Collings, the oldest personal friend of Maltby's father, studied Maltby's face for several seconds and then walked into the radio room. He was pale when he came back. "He refuses to come up here. He says if you want to see him you can come down. Peter, this is outrageous."

"Tell him," said Maltby steadily, "that I'll be right down."

He smiled at their dour faces. "Gentlemen," he said in a ringing tone, "this man is playing into our hands. Broadcast that I'm going down for the sake of amity in a great crisis. Don't overdo it, but put just a hint of doubt into your announcement, indicating that possibly violence will be done me."

He finished matter-of-factly: "Obviously, nothing will

happen, with this ship floating here in a dominant position. However, if I'm not back in an hour and a half, try to contact me. Then, step by step, beginning with threats, reach the point where you start shooting."

Despite his confidence, he had a curious feeling of emptiness and aloneness as his lifeboat settled down on the roof of Hunston's headquarters.

Hunston was a tall, sardonic-looking man in his middle thirties. As Maltby entered his private office, he stood up, came forward, and shook hands. He said in a quiet, pleasant voice: "I wanted to get you away from those wet hens who rule the roost down here. No *lese majesty* was intended. I want to talk to you. I think I can convince you."

He made the attempt in a low, cultured but very alive voice. His arguments were the stale arguments of the basic superiority of the Mixed Men. He obviously believed his own premises, and in the end Maltby could not escape the conviction that the man's main fault was lack of general and specific information about the world outside. He had lived too long in this narrow environment of the Mixed Men cities, spent too many years talking and thinking without reference to larger realities. Despite his brilliance, Hunston was provincially minded.

The rebel leader completed his monologue, and asked a question: "Do you believe that the Fifty Suns will be able to remain hidden from Earth civilization?"

"No," said Maltby truthfully. "I believe eventual discovery is inevitable."

"Yet you support their deluded attempt to remain secret?"

"I support unity in dealing with the situation. I believe it is wise to be cautious in accepting contact. It is even possible that we could hold off discovery for a hundred years, perhaps longer."

Hunston was silent. There was a scowl on his handsome face. "I can see," he said at last, "that we hold opposite views."

Watching the man, Maltby said slowly: "Perhaps our

longrun intentions are the same. Perhaps we merely have different plans for arriving at the same goal."

Hunston's face lighted; his eyes widened slightly. He said eagerly: "Your excellency, if I could believe that." He broke off, his eyes narrowing abruptly: "I'd like to hear your opinion of the future role of the Mixed Men in civilization."

"Given the opportunity, using legal methods," said Maltby quietly, "they will inevitably gravitate towards positions of top leadership. Without taking unfair advantage of their ability to control others mentally, they will first dominate the Fifty Suns, and then the main galaxy. If at any time in their rise to power, they use force, they will be destroyed to the last man, woman and child."

Hunston's eyes were bright. "And how long do you think it will take?" he asked.

"It can begin in your lifetime and mine. It will require at least a thousand years, depending on how rapidly Dellians and human beings intermarry—as of now, children are forbidden in such marriages, as you know—"

Hunston nodded scowling; then he said: "I have been misinformed about your attitude. You are one of us."

"No!" Maltby spoke firmly. "Please do not confuse a long-run with a short-term attitude. It's the difference in this case between life and death. Even to mention that we expect in the end to gain domination would alarm people who have now been prepared by their governments to be cautiously friendly. If we show our unity regarding this issue, we can make a beginning. If we are opportunistic, then this little race of supermen of which you and I are members will sooner or later be destroyed."

Hunston was on his feet. "Your excellency, I'll accept that. I'll go along with you. We'll await developments."

It was an unexpected victory for him who had come prepared to use force. Despite his belief, however, that Hunston was sincere, he had no intention of merely taking the other's word. The man might change his mind as soon as the threat of the *Atmion* was removed. He said so, frankly, and finished: "Under the circumstances, I'll have to ask you to submit to a six months term of imprisonment at some point where you cannot be in touch with your supporters. It will be merely a form of house arrest. You can take your wife. You will receive every courtesy; and will be freed immediately if contact is established in the meantime between the Earth ship and the Fifty Suns. Your position will be that of hostage rather than prisoner. I'll give you twenty-four hours to think it over."

No attempt was made to stop him as he returned to his lifeboat, and so back to the warship.

Hunston surrendered himself at the end of the 24-hour period. He specified one condition: the terms of his house arrest must be broadcast.

And so the Fifty Suns were safe from immediate discovery, it being obvious that one ship could not without aid find even one planet of so well-hidden a civilization. Maltby was convinced of it. There remained the problem of the inevitable discovery when other ships came from the main galaxy a few years hence. Curiously, now that the main danger was over, that began to worry him. As he guided the Fifty Suns' battleship *Atmion* back up its original course, Maltby considered just what he might do to insure further the safety of the people of the Greater Magellanic Cloud.

Somebody, it seemed to him, ought to find out just how great the danger was. The mere notion of how that would have to be done made him shaky; and yet, with each passing hour, he found himself becoming more determined, and more convinced that he with his good will was the one person best suited to do the job.

He was still considering how he might let his ship be captured when the alarms began to sound.

"Lady Laurr, we have established upper resonance contact with a vessel of this system."

"Seize it!"

Chapter Six

JUST how it was done, Maltby had no clear idea. In the early stages of the capture, he was too willing to be caught. By the time tractor beams gripped the *Atmion* it was a little late to analyze how the invader ship had maneuvered his own craft into the tractor beam field.

Something happened, a physical sensation of being sucked into a vortex, a perceived tension and contortion of his own body, as if the basic matter of which he was composed was being subjected to strain. Whatever it was ended abruptly as the tractors took hold, and the Fifty Suns' battleship was drawn towards the remote darkness where the other ship lay to, still hidden by distance.

Anxiously, Maltby watched the measuring instruments that might give him some estimate of the other vessel's size. As the minutes sped by, he began to realize it was improbable he would actually see the enemy machine. In that vast night, even nearby suns were dim points of light. The characteristics of any body out here could only be determined over a period of time. Anything as small as a ship was like a dust mote lost in inconceivable darkness.

His doubts were realized. When the *Atmion* was still several light-minutes from its captor, a sharp, tortuous pain twisted his muscles. He had time to guess: paralyzer ray. And then, he was writhing on the floor of the control room, with darkness closing over him.

He woke up, tense, wary, convinced that he had to seize control of the situation, whatever it might be. He guessed that there would be methods for controlling his mind, and forcing it to give information. He must even assume that his own powerful double brain could be over-come, once its potentialities were suspected.

He opened his eyes ever so slightly by relaxing the muscles of the eyelids. It was as if he had given a signal. From somewhere nearby a man said in an odd but un-derstandable English:

"All right, ease her through the lock."

Maltby closed his eyes, but not before he had recog-nized that he was still inside the *Atmion*. And that appar-ently the process of taking the Fifty Suns' battleship into the captor machine was just under way. The fact that he was still lying where he had fallen in the control room seemed to indicate that the officers and crew of the *At-mion* had not yet been questioned.

A wave of excitement swept through him. Was it going to be as simple as that? Was it possible that all he need do was probe cautiously with his two minds—and take con-trol of any human being he contacted? And thus take con-trol of the boarding crew? Was all that going to be possible?

It was. It happened.

Maltby was herded with the others along a corridor that stretched into the distance ahead. Armed crew mem-bers of the Earth ship—both men and women—walked ahead and behind the long line of captives.

It was an illusion. The real prisoners were the officers in charge of the prisoners. At the proper moment, the com-mander—a sturdy young man of forty or so—quietly ordered the main body of captives to continue along the corridor. But Maltby and the other officers from Astroga-tion and Meteorology were taken down a side corridor, and into a large apartment with half a dozen bedrooms.

The Earth officer said matter-of-factly, "You'll be all right here. We'll bring proper uniforms, and you can move around the ship whenever you wish—provided you don't talk to our people too much. We've got all kinds of dialects aboard, but none quite like yours. We don't want you to be noticed, so watch yourselves!"

Maltby was not worried. His problem, as he saw it, was to familiarize himself with the ship and its procedures. It was already obvious that it was a huge vessel, and that there were more people aboard than one man could ever control directly. He suspected that there also were traps for the unwary intruder. But that was something that had to be risked. Once he had a general picture of the ship and its departments, he would quickly explore the unknown dangers.

When the "captors" had gone, he joined the other astrogation men in a raid on the kitchen. As he had half-anticipated, there were many similarities in food. The Dellian and non-Dellian humanoids had brought domesticated animals with them millenia ago. And now here in these deep freezers were steer steaks, pork and lamb chops, roasts and an enormous variety of Earth-origin fowl, each in its airtight transparent wrapper.

The men ate to satiation; and Maltby discussed in serious vein with them the mystery of why they were being treated as they were. He was acutely conscious of the fact that he had done a dangerous thing. There were sharp minds present; and if one of them ever made a connection between what had happened and the fear the Fifty Suns people had of the Mixed Men, his report might well frighten his superiors more than had the Earth ship. He was relieved when the officer he controlled came back with a supply of uniforms.

The problem of control in front of Fifty Suns' men was a delicate one. It involved the "slave" believing that he was doing what he was for a rational reason. The reason the man had accepted was that he was acting under orders to win the good will of the most valuable officers on the captured ship. He had the impression, moreover, that it would be unwise to communicate this information directly to his charges, and that he must not discuss it with brother officers of the ship.

As a result he was quite prepared to supply the indoctrination that would enable Maltby and the others to move in a limited fashion about the *Star Cluster*. He was not prepared to give them too much data about the ship itself. So long as the others were present, Maltby accepted the limitation. But it was he who accompanied the officer

when the latter, feeling his job done, finally departed.
To Maltby's chagrin, the man proved invulnerable to
mind control when it came to information about the ship.
He was willing, but he *couldn't* impart that kind of data.
Something—some suppressor on him, perhaps hypnotic in
nature—prevented. It seemed clear, finally, that Maltby
would have to learn what he wanted to know from higher
officers who had freedom of choice. Lower rank officers
obviously did not, and the method used to protect them
was one that he couldn't take the time to analyze and
overcome.

He guessed that the ship's authorities would by now be
discovering that *Atmion's* astrogators and meterologists
were missing. Somebody would be concerned about that
in the determined and grim fashion of the military mind.
If only he could get a chance to talk to the woman who
was commander-in-chief of the Earth ship . . . But that in
itself would make other steps essential. Escape?

Though it was important that he waste no time, it
nevertheless required two hours more to control the
officers who had charge of the captured Fifty Suns people
and of the *Atmion*—to control them in such a way that, at
a given signal, they would coordinate their actions and
arrange an escape. In each case it was necessary to produce an actual or hallucinatory command from a superior officer in order to obtain the automatic acquies-
cence of the individual. As a precaution, Maltby also provided the explanation that the *Atmion* was to be released
as a friendly gesture to the Fifty Suns Government.

That done, he successfully conveyed to a top officer
that the Grand Captain insisted on seeing him. Just how
it would all work out, Maltby had only the vaguest idea.

Lieutenant Neslor came into the bridge, and deposited
her gaunted body in a chair. She sighed. "Something is
wrong," she said.

The Grand Captain turned from what she had been
doing at the control board, and studied the older woman
thoughtfully. She shrugged finally with a hint of anger
in her manner, and said in irritation: "Surely, some of
these Fifty Suns people know where their planets are."

The psychologist shook her head. "We have found no astrogation officers aboard. The other prisoners were as surprised at that as I was."

Lady Laurr frowned. "I don't think I understand." She spoke slowly.

"There are five of them," said Lieutenant Neslor. "All were seen a few minutes before we captured the *Atmion*. Now, they're missing."

The younger woman said quickly: "Search the ship! Sound a general attention!" She half-turned back to the great instrument board, and then stopped herself. Thoughtfully, she faced the psychologist. "I see you don't consider that is the method."

"We're already had one experience with a Dellian," was the reply.

The Lady Gloria shuddered slightly. The memory of Gisser Watcher, the man who had been captured on the meteorite station, was still not completely resolved within her. She said finally, "What do you suggest?"

"Wait! They must have had a plan, whatever method they used to escape our energy control. I'd like to see where they try to go, what they want to find out."

"I see." The Grand Captain made no other comment. She seemed to be gazing far away.

"Naturally," said Lieutenant Neslor, "you'll have to be protected. I'll make that my personal task."

Lady Laurr shrugged. "I really can't imagine how a newcomer aboard this ship could ever hope to find my apartment. If I should ever forget the method, I wouldn't care to have to figure out how to get back here." She broke off. "Is that all you have to suggest? Just wait and see what happens?"

"That's all."

The young woman shook her head. "That's not enough for me, my dear. I'm assuming that my earlier commands about precautions have been taken, and are still in force." She turned abruptly to the control board. A moment later a face came on the plate. "Ah, Captain," said Gloria, "what are your police doing right now?"

"Searching and guarding," was the reply.

"Any success?"

"The ship is completely guarded against accidental explosions. All bombs are accounted for, with remote control observers watching key entrances. No surprise is possible."

"Good," said Grand Captain Laurr. "Carry on." She broke the connection and yawned. "I guess it's bedtime. I'll be seeing you, my dear."

Lieutenant Neslor stood up. "I feel fairly sure that you can sleep safely."

She went out. The younger woman spent half an hour dictating memos to various departments, adjusting for each one the time at which it should be communicated. Presently, she undressed and went to bed. She was asleep almost at once.

She awakened with an odd sense of dissatisfaction. Except for the ever so faint glow from the instrument board, the bridge was in darkness, but after a moment she thought in amazement: "There's someone in the room."

She lay very still, savoring the menace, and remembering what Lieutenant Neslor had said. It seemed incredible that anyone unfamiliar with this monstrously large vessel should have located her so quickly. Her eyes were becoming accustomed to the darkness now, and in that dimness she was able to make out the silhouette of a man standing a few feet from her bed.

He must have been waiting for her to discover him. He must have been aware, somehow, that she was awake, for he said: "Don't turn on the light. And be very careful."

His voice was soft, almost gentle; yet it convinced her that the speaker was an extremely dangerous man. His command held her in the bed, and kept her hand where it was on the sheet, unmoving. It even brought the first anguish of fear, the realization that before any help could reach her she might die. She could only hope that Lieutenant Neslor was awake, and watching.

The intruder spoke again: "Nothing will happen to you if you do exactly as I say."

"*Who are you?*" Her tone conveyed her will to know.

Maltby did not answer. He had located a chair now, and he settled himself into it, but he was not happy with his situation. There were too many mechanical devices aboard a battleship for him to feel any sense of security in what he was doing. He could be defeated, even destroyed, without warning. He could imagine that, even now, the scene was under observation from some remote source beyond his power to control. He said slowly, "Madam, nothing will happen to you if you yourself make no overt moves. I'm here with the hope of having a few questions answered. To ease your mind, I am one of the astrogators of the Fifty Suns' ship, *Atmion*. I won't go into the details of how we escaped your net, but I'm here talking to you this way because of your propaganda. You were right in thinking that there are differences of opinion among the people of the Fifty Suns. Some feel that we should accept your assurances. Others are afraid. Naturally, the fearful ones being in the majority have won. It always seems safer to wait and hope."

He paused, and went back over his words with his mind's ear; and, though he could have worded them better—so it seemed to him—they sounded right in essence. If the people of this ship could ever be persuaded to believe anything he might say at this moment, it would be that he and others like him were still undecided. Maltby continued in the same careful, unhurried vein: "I represent a group that occupies a unique position in this affair. Only the astrogators and meteorologists on the various planets and ships are able to communicate the position of inhabited worlds. There are probably tens of thousands of would-be-traitors who would betray their people in a moment for personal gain, but they are not among the trained and disciplined personnel of the government or the forces. I'm sure you will understand well what that means." He paused again, to give her time to understand it.

The woman had relaxed gradually, as Maltby talked. His words sounded rational, his intentions strange but not unbelievable. What bothered her was almost tiny by comparison: How had he found his way to her apartment? Anyone less familiar than she with the intricacies of the ship's operation might have accepted the reality of his presence, and let it go at that. But she knew the laws of chance that were involved. It was as if he had come into a strange city of thirty thousand inhabitants, and—without previous knowledge—walked straight to the home of the person he wanted to see. She shook her head ever so slightly, rejecting the explanation. She waited, nevertheless, for him to continue. His words had already reassured her as to her safety, and every moment that passed would make it more certain that Lieutenant Neslor was on the job. She might even learn something.

Maltby said: "We have to have some information. The decision you are trying to force upon us is one that we should all like to postpone. For us, it would be so much simpler if you would return to the main galaxy, and send other ships back here at some later date. Then there would be time to adjust to the inevitable, and no one need be in the unenviable position of having to think of betraying his people."

Gloria nodded, in the darkness. This she could understand. She said: "What questions do you want answered?"

"How long have you been in the Greater Magellanic Cloud?"

"Ten years."

Maltby went on: "How much longer do you plan to stay?"

"That information is not available," said the Grand Captain, her voice steady. It struck her that the statement was true even so far as she herself was concerned. The plebiscite would not take place for two days.

Maltby said, "I strongly advise that you answer my questions."

"What will happen if I don't?"

As she spoke, her hand, which she had moved carefully toward a small instrument board at the edge of her bed, attained its goal. Triumphantly, she pressed one of the buttons. She relaxed instantly. Out the darkness Maltby said: "I decided to let you do that. I hope it makes you feel more secure."

His calmness disconcerted her, but she wondered if he understood clearly what she had done. Coolly, she explained that she had activated a bank of what was known as sensitive lights. From this moment on, they would watch him with their numerous electronic eyes. Any attempt on his part to use an energy weapon would be met by counteracting forces. It also prevented her from using a weapon, but it seemed unwise to mention that.

Maltby said, "I have no intention of using an energy weapon. But I'd like you to answer more questions."

"I might." She spoke mildly, but she was beginning to be irritated with Lieutenant Neslor. Surely, some action was now indicated.

Maltby said, "How big a ship is this?"

"It's fifteen hundred feet long, and carries a complement of three thousand officers and lower ranks."

"That's pretty big," said Maltby. He was impressed and wondered how much she was exaggerating.

The Grand Captain made no comment. The real size was ten times what she had stated. But it wasn't size that counted so much as the quality of what was inside. She felt fairly sure that this interrogator had not even begun to understand how tremendous was the defensive and offensive potential of the vast ship she commanded. Only a few higher officers understood the nature of some of the forces that could be brought into play. At the moment those officers were supposed to be under constant surveillance by remote-control observers.

Maltby said: "I'm puzzled as to just how we were captured. Could you explain that to me?"

So he had finally came around to that. Lady Laurr raised her voice: "Lieutenant Neslor."

"Yes, noble lady." The reply came promptly from somewhere in the darkness.

"Don't you think this comedy has gone on long enough?"

"I do indeed. Shall I kill him?"

"No. I want *him* to answer some questions."

Maltby took control of her mind, as he walked hurriedly to the transmitter. Behind him—

"Don't fire!" said Gloria in an intense voice. "Let him go!"

Even afterwards, she did not seriously question that command, or the impulse that had driven her to say it. Her explanation to herself—later—was that since the intruder had not threatened her, and since he was one of the much-wanted astrogators, to destroy him in order to prevent his escaping to some other part of the ship would be an irrational act.

As a result Maltby left the bridge safely and was able to give the signal that freed the *Atmion*. As the Fifty Suns' vessel fled into the distance, the officers of the Earth ship—acting on a final cue from him—began to forget their share in the escape.

Mentally, that was as far as Maltby had gotten. To enter the enemy vessel and to get away again—it had seemed a big enough venture in itself. What he had learned was not altogether satisfactory, but he did know they were dealing with a very large vessel. It was a vessel that would have to be careful in its dealings with a fleet, but he did not doubt that it had weapons capable of destroying several Fifty Suns' battleships at the same time.

What bothered him was, how would the officers and crew of the *Atmion*, and the Fifty Suns' people in general, react to the incident? That seemed too complex for any one man to calculate. And as for what would happen aboard the *Star Cluster*—that was even more difficult to forecast.

All the reactions did not show immediately. Maltby was aware that Admiral Dreehan made a report to the Fifty Suns government. But for two days nothing occurred.

On the third day, the *Star Cluster's* daily broadcast of its course showed that it had drastically altered its direction. The reason for the change was obscure.

On the fourth day, Maltby's viewplate lighted with the image of Vice-admiral Dreehan. The commanding officer said gravely: "This is a general announcement to all ranks. I have just received the following message from the military headquarters of our fleet."

Quietly, he read the message.

"It is hereby declared that a state of war exists between the peoples of the Fifty Suns and the Earth ship *Star Cluster*. The fleet shall place itself in the path of the enemy, and seek battle. Ships incapacitated and in danger of capture must destroy their star maps; and all meteorological and astrogation officers aboard such vessels are patriotically required to commit suicide. It is the declared policy of the sovereign government of the Fifty Suns that the invader must be destroyed."

Maltby listened, pale and tense, as Dreehan went on in a more conversational tone: "I have private information that the government has drawn the conclusion from our experience, that the *Star Cluster* released us because they dared not rouse the anger of our people. From this and other data, the leaders have decided that the Earth ship can be destroyed by a determined attack. If we dutifully follow the exact instructions we have received, then even the capture of individual ships will give the enemy no advantage. I have already appointed executioners for all Meteorological and Astrogation officers in the event that they cannot act for themselves at the crucial moment, so please take note."

Captain Peter Maltby, chief meteorologist of the *Atmion*, and an assistant astrogator, noted with a sick awareness that he was committed. He had laid down a policy of united action with the people of the Fifty Suns. It was out of the question that he, for personal reasons, now hastily abandon that attitude.

His only hope was that the wolves of space—as the warships were often called—would by pack action make short work of the single Earth ship.

They ran into a tiger.

Chapter Seven

SHE had lost the plebiscite by a heart-breaking nine to ten vote. Grimly, she ordered the big ship to alter course for home.

Late that "day," Communication called her: "Shall we continue to broadcast our course?"

At least, she still had control over that. "Most certainly," she said curtly.

The following afternoon, she awakened from a nap to the sound of alarm bells ringing.

"Thousands of ships ahead!" reported Captain chief of operations.

"Slow for action!" she commanded. "Battle stations."

When that was done, and their speed was less than a thousand miles a second, she spoke to the captains in council.

"Well, sirs and ladies," she said with unconcealed delight, "I should like to have authorization to wage battle against a recalcitrant government, which is now showing that it is capable of taking the most hostile action against Earth civilization."

"Gloria," said one of the women, "please don't rub it in. This is one of your times for being right."

The vote to accept battle was unanimous. Afterwards, the question was asked:

"Are we going to destroy them, or capture them?"

"Capture."

"All of them?"

"All."

When the Fifty Suns fleet and the Earth ship were

some four hundred million miles apart, the *Star Cluster* set up a field that took in a vast section of space.

It was a miniature universe, intensely curved. Ships pursuing an apparently straight course found themselves circling back to their original positions. Attempts to break out of the trap by attaining velocities in excess of light-speed proved futile. A shower of torpedoes directed at the source of the field veered off and had to be exploded in space to avoid damaging their own ships.

It was found impossible to communicate with any planets of the Fifty Suns. Sub-space radio was as silent as death.

At the end of about four hours, the *Star Cluster* set up a series of tractor beams. One by one, inexorably, ships were drawn towards the giant battleship.

It was at that time that stern orders were issued for all Fifty Suns' meteorological and astrogation officers to commit suicide at once.

On the *Atmion* Maltby was one of a pale group of men who shook hands with Vice-admiral Dreehan; and immediately afterwards, in the commanding officer's presence, pointed a blaster at the side of his head.

At that penultimate moment, he hesitated. "I could take control of him now, this instant—and save my life."

He told himself angrily that the whole affair was futile and unnecessary. Discovery of the Fifty Suns had been inevitable in the sense that it would occur sooner or later, regardless of what he did now.

And then, he thought: "This is what I've stood for among the Mixed Men. We must be one with the group, to death, if necessary."

His brief hesitation ended. He touched the activator of his weapon.

As the first captured ships were boarded by teams of technicians, the exultant young woman on the bridge of the greatest ship that had ever entered the Greater Magellanic Cloud learned of the suicides.

Pity touched her. "Revive them all!" she ordered. "There is no need for anyone to die."

"Some of them are pretty badly splattered," was the answer. "They used blasters."

She frowned at that. It meant an immense amount of extra work. "The fools!" she said. "They almost deserve death."

She broke off. "Use extra care! If necessary, put whole ships through the matter transmitter with emphasis on synthesis of damaged tissues and organs."

Far into the sleep period, she sat at her desk receiving reports. Several revived astrogators were brought before her; and, with the help of Lieutenant Neslor, of Psychology, she questioned them.

Before she retired to sleep, a lost civilization had been found.

Chapter Eight

OVER the miles and the years, the gases drifted. Waste matter from ten thousand suns, a diffuse miasm of spent explosions, of dead hell fires and the furies of a hundred million raging sunspots—formless, purposeless.

But it was the beginning.

Into the great dark the gases crept. Calcium was in them, and sodium, and hydrogen; most of the elements, and the speed of the drift varied up to twenty miles a second.

There was a timeless period while gravitation performed its function. The inchoate mass became masses. Great blobs of gas took semblance of shape in widely separate areas, and moved on and on and on.

They came finally to where a thousand flaring seetee suns had long before doggedly "crossed the street" of the main stream of terrene suns. Had crossed, and left *their* excrement and gases.

The first clash quickened the vast worlds of gas. The electron haze of terrene plunged like spurred horses and sped deeper into the equally violently reacting positron haze of contraterrene. Instantly, the lighter orbital positrons and electrons went up in a blaze of hard radiation.

The storm was on.

The stripped seetee nuclei carried now terrific and unbalanced negative charges and repelled electrons, but tended to attract terrene atom nuclei. In their turn the stripped terrene nuclei attracted contraterrene.

Violent beyond all conception were the resulting cancellations of charges. The two opposing masses heaved and spun in a cataclysm of partial adjustment. They had been heading in different directions. More and more they became one tangled, seething whirlpool.

The new course, uncertain at first, steadied; then, on a front of nine light years, at a solid fraction of the velocity of light, the storm roared toward its destiny.

Suns were engulfed for a half a hundred years—and left behind with only a hammering of cosmic rays to show that they had been the centers of otherwise invisible, impalpable atomic devastation.

In its four hundred and ninetieth Sidereal year, the storm intersected the orbit of a Nova at the flash moment.

It began to move!

On the three dimensional map at weather headquarters on the planet Kaider III, the storm was colored orange. Which meant it was the biggest of the four hundred odd storms raging in the Fifty Suns region of the Greater Magellanic Cloud.

It showed as an uneven splotch fronting at Latitude 473, Longitude 228, Center 190 parsecs. But that was a special Fifty Suns degree system which had no relation to the magnetic center of the Magellanic Cloud as a whole.

The report about the Nova had not yet been registered on the map. When that happened, the storm color would be changed to an angry red.

They had stopped looking at the map. Maltby stood with the councilors at the great window, staring up at the Earth ship.

The machine was scarcely more than a dark sliver in the distant sky. But the sight of it seemed to hold a deadly fascination for the older men.

Maltby felt cool, determined, but also sardonic. It was funny, these—these people of the Fifty Suns in this hour of their danger calling upon *him*.

He unfocused his eyes from the ship, fixed his steely gaze on the plump, perspiring chairman of the Kaider III government—and, tensing his mind, forced the man to look at him. The councilor, unaware of the compulsion, conscious only that he had turned, said, "You understand your instructions, Captain Maltby?"

Maltby nodded. "I do."

It was more than that. He accepted their attitude, their purpose, as part and parcel of his belief that only the fullest cooperation would enable the Mixed Men to take their place safely in the culture from which they had sprung. At this late hour, the resistance of the Fifty Suns was a forlorn hope. And yet, it was not for him as an officer to question their logic.

The curt reply must have evoked a vivid picture. The fat face rippled like palsied jelly and broke out in a new trickle of sweat. He said, "Captain Maltby, you must not fail. They have asked for a meteorologist to guide them to Cassidor VII, where the central government is located. They mustn't reach there. You must drive them into the great storm at 473. We have commissioned you to do this for us because you have the two minds of the Mixed Men. We regret that we have not always fully appreciated your services in the past. But you must admit that, after the wars of the Mixed Men, it was natural that we should be careful about—"

Maltby cut off the lame apology. "Forget it," he said. "The Mixed Men are as deeply involved, as I see it, as the Dellians and non-Dellians. I assure you I shall do my best to wreck this ship."

"Be careful!" the chairman urged anxiously. "It could destroy us, our planet, our sun in a single minute. We never dreamed that Earth could have gotten so far ahead of us and produced such a devastatingly powerful machine. After all, the non-Dellians and, of course, the Mixed Men among us are capable of research work; the former have been laboring feverishly for thousands of years. And, finally, remember that you are not being asked to commit suicide. The battleship is invincible. Just how it will survive a real storm we were not told when we were being shown around. But it will. What happens, however, is that everyone aboard becomes unconscious. As a Mixed Man you will be the first to revive. Our combined fleets, which as you know have been released, will be waiting to board the ship the moment you advise us. Is that clear?"

It had been clear the first time it had been explained, but these non-Dellians had a habit of repeating themselves, as if thoughts kept growing vague in their minds. As Maltby closed the door of the great room behind him, one of the councilors said to his neighbor:

"Has he been told that the storm has gone Nova?"

The fat man overheard. He shook his head. His eyes gleamed as he said quietly, "No. After all, he is one of the Mixed Men. We can't trust him too far, no matter what his record."

Chapter Nine

ALL morning the reports had come in. Some showed progress, some didn't. But her basic good humor was untouched by the failures. The great reality was that her luck had held. The information she wanted was coming in: Population of Kaider III two billion, one hundred million, two-fifths Dellian, three fifths non-Dellian. The former were so-called robots.

Dellians were physically and mentally the higher type, but they lacked creative ability. Non-Dellians dominated in the research laboratories. The forty-nine other suns whose planets were inhabited were called, in alphabetical order. Assora, Atmion, Bresp, Buraco, Cassidor, Corrab— They were located at (1) Assora: Latitude 931, Longitude 27, Center 201 parsecs; (2) Atmion—

It went on and on. Just before noon she noted with steely amusement that there was still nothing coming through from meteorology, nothing at all about storms. She made the proper connection and flung her words: "What's the matter, Lieutenant Cannons? Your assistants have been making prints and duplicates of various Kaider maps. Aren't you getting anything?"

The old meteorologist shook his head. "You will recall, noble lady, that when we captured that robot in space, he had time to send out a warning. Immediately, on every Fifty Suns planet, all maps were destroyed, commercial spaceships were stripped of radios capable of sub-space communication, and they received orders to go to a planet on a chance basis, and stay there until further notice. To my mind, all this was done before it was clearly grasped that their navy hadn't a chance against us. Now they are going to provide us with a meteorologist, but we shall have to depend on our lie detectors as to whether or not he is telling us the truth."

"I see." The woman smiled, "Have no fear. They don't dare oppose us openly. No doubt there is a plan being built up against us, but it cannot prevail now that we can take action to enforce our unalterable will. Whomever they send must tell us the truth. Let me know when he comes."

Lunch came, but she ate at her desk, watching the flashing pictures on the astro, listening to the murmur of voices, storing the facts, the general picture, into her brain.

"There's no doubt, Captain Turgess," she commenced once, savagely, "that we're being lied to on a vast scale. But let it be so. We can use psychological tests to verify all the vital details. For the time being it is important that you relieve the fears of everyone you find it necessary to question. We must convince these people that Earth will accept them on an equal basis without bias or prejudice of any kind because of their robot orig—" She bit her lip. "That's an ugly word, the worst kind of propaganda. We must eliminate it from our thoughts."

"I'm afraid," the officer shrugged, "not from our thoughts."

She stared at him, narrow eyed, then cut him off angrily. A moment later she was talking into the general transmitter: "The word robot must not be used—by any of our personnel—under pain of fine—"

Switching off, she put a busy signal on her spare receiver, and called Psychology House. Lieutenant Neslor's face appeared on the plate.

"I heard your order just now, noble lady," the woman psychologist said. "I'm afraid, however, that we're dealing with the deepest instincts of the human animal—hatred or fear of the stranger, the alien. Excellency, we come from a long line of ancestors, who, in their time, have felt superior to others because of some slight variation in the pigmentation of the skin. It is even recorded that the color of the eyes has influenced the egoistic in historical decisions. We have sailed into very deep waters, and it will be the crowning achievement of our life if we sail out in a satisfactory fashion."

There was an eager lilt in the psychologist's voice; and the grand captain experienced a responsive thrill of joy. If there was one thing she appreciated, it was the positive outlook, the kind of people who faced all obstacles short of the recognizably impossible with a youthful zest, a will to win. She was still smiling as she broke the connection.

The high thrill sagged. She sat cold with her problem. It was a problem. Hers. All aristocratic officers had *carte blanche* powers, and were expected to resolve difficulties involving anything up to whole groups of planetary systems.

After a minute she dialed the meteorology room again. "Lieutenant Cannons, when the meteorology officer of the Fifty Suns navy arrives, please employ the following tactics—"

Maltby waved dismissal to the driver of his car. The machine pulled away from the curb and Maltby stood frowning at the flaming energy barrier that barred further progress along the street. Finally he took another look at the Earth ship.

It was directly above him now that he had come so many miles across the city toward it. It was tremendously high up, a long, black torpedo shape almost lost in the mist of distance. But high as it was it was still visibly bigger than anything ever seen by the Fifty Suns, an incredible creation of metal from a world so far away that, almost, it had sunk to the status of a myth.

Here was the reality. There would be tests, he thought, penetrating tests before they'd accept any orbit he planned. It wasn't that he doubted the ability of his double mind to overcome anything like that, but it was well to remember that the frightful gap of years which separated the science of Earth from that of the Fifty Suns had already shown unpleasant surprises. Maltby shook himself grimly and gave his full attention to the street ahead.

A fan-shaped pink fire spread skyward from two machines that stood in the center of the street. The flame was a very pale pink and completely transparent. It looked electronic, deadly. Beyond it were men in glittering uniforms. A steady trickle of them moved in and out of buildings. About three blocks down the avenue a second curtain of pink fire flared up.

There seemed to be no attempt to guard the sides. The men he could see looked at ease, confident. There was murmured conversations, low laughter and—as he had observed when he was previously aboard the *Star Cluster*, they weren't all men. As Maltby walked forward, two fine-looking women in uniform came down the steps of the nearest of the requisitioned buildings. One of the guards of the flame said something to them. There was a twin tinkle of silvery laughter. Still laughing, they strode off down the street.

It was suddenly exciting. There was an air about these people of far places, of tremendous and wonderful lands beyond the farthest horizons of the staid Fifty Suns. He felt cold, then hot, then he glanced up at the fantastically big ship; and the chill came back. One ship, he thought, but so big, so mighty that the fleet of thirty billion people had been helpless against it. They—

He grew aware that one of the brilliantly arrayed guards was staring at him. The man spoke into a wrist radio, and after a moment, a second man broke off his conversation with a third soldier and came over. He stared through the flame barrier at Maltby.

"Is there anything you desire? Or are you just looking?" His manner was mild, almost gentle, cultured. The whole effect had a naturalness, an unalienness that was pleasing. After all, Maltby thought, he had no fear of these people. His very plan to defeat the ship was based upon his own fundamental belief that the robots were indestructible in the sense that no one could ever wipe them out completely.

Quietly, Maltby explained his presence.

"Oh yes," the man nodded, "we've been expecting you. I'm to take you at once to the meteorological room of the ship. Just a moment—"

The flame barrier went down and Maltby was led into one of the buildings. There was a long corridor, and the transmitter that projected him into the ship must have been focused somewhere along it. Because abruptly he was in a very large room. Maps floated in half a dozen antigravity pits. The walls shed light from millions of tiny point sources. And everywhere were tables with curved lines of very dim but sharply etched light on their surfaces.

Maltby's guide was nowhere to be seen. Coming toward him, however, was a tall, fine-looking old man. The oldster offered his hand.

"My name is Cannons, senior ship meteorologist. If you will sit down here we can plan an orbit and the ship can get under way within the hour. The grand captain is very anxious that we get started."

Maltby nodded casually. But he was stiff, alert. He stood quite still, feeling around with that acute second mind of his, his Dellian mind, for energy pressures that would show secret attempts to watch or control his mind.

But there was nothing like that. He smiled tautly. It was going to be as simple as this, was it? Like hell it was.

Chapter Ten

AS HE sat down, Maltby felt suddenly cozy and alive. The exhilaration of existence burned through him like a flame. He recognized the excitement for the battle thrill it was, and felt joy that he could do something about it.

During his long service in the Fifty Suns navy he had faced hostility and suspicion because he was a Mixed Man. And always he felt helpless. Now, here was a far more basic hostility, however veiled, and a suspicion that must be like a burning fire. And this time he could fight. He could look this skillfully voluble, friendly old man squarely in the eye and—

Friendly?

"It makes me smile sometimes," the old man was saying, "when I think of the unscientific aspects of the orbit we have to plan now. For instance, what is the time lag on storm reports out here?"

Maltby could not repress a smile. So Lieutenant Cannons wanted to know things, did he? To give the man credit, it wasn't really a lame opening. The truth was, the only way to ask a question was—well—to ask it.

Maltby said: "Oh, three, four months. Nothing unusual. Each space meteorologist takes about that length of time to check the bounds of the particular storm in his area, and then reports, and we adjust our maps. Fortunately"—he pushed his second mind to the fore as he coolly spoke the great basic lie—"there are no major storms between the Kaidor and Cassidor suns."

He continued, sliding over the untruth like an eel breasting wet rock: "However, several suns prevent a straight line movement. So if you would show me some

of your orbits for twenty-five hundred light years, I'll
make a selection of the best ones."

He wasn't, he realized instantly, going to slip over his
main point as easily as that.

"No intervening storms?" the old man said. He pursed
his lips. The fine lines in his long face seemed to deepen.
He looked genuinely nonplused; and there was no doubt
at all that he hadn't expected such a straightforward statement. "Hm-m-m, no storms. That does make it simple,
doesn't it?"

He broke off. "You know, the important thing about
two"—he hesitated over the word, then went on—"two
people, who have been brought up in different cultures,
under different scientific stardards, is that they make sure
they are discussing a subject from a common viewpoint.
Space is so big. Even this comparatively small system of
stars, the Greater Magellanic Cloud, is so vast that it
defies our reason. We on the battleship *Star Cluster* have
spent ten years surveying it, and now we are able to say
glibly that it comprises two hundred millions of suns. We
located the magnetic center of the Cloud, fixed our zero
line from center to the great brightest star, S Doradus;
and now, I suppose, there are people who would be fools
enough to think we've got the system stowed away in
our brainpans."

Maltby was silent, because he himself was just such a
fool. This was warning. He was being told in no uncertain terms that they were in a position to check any orbit
he gave them with respect to all intervening suns.

It meant much more. It showed that Earth was on the
verge of extending her tremendous sway to the Greater
Magellanic Cloud. Destroying this ship now would provide the Fifty Suns with precious years during which
they would have to decide what they intended to do.

But that would be all. Other ships would come; the
inexorable pressure of the stupendous populations of the
main galaxy would burst out even farther into space.
Always under careful control, shepherded by mighty
hosts of invincible battleships, the great transports would
sweep into the Cloud, and every planet everywhere would

acknowledge Earth suzerainty. Imperial Earth recognized no separate nations of any description anywhere. Dellian, non-Dellian and Mixed Men would need every extra day, every hour; and it was lucky for them all that he was not basing his hope of destroying this ship on an orbit that would end inside a sun.

Their survey had magnetically placed all the suns for them. But they couldn't know about the storms. Not in ten years or in a hundred was it possible for one ship to locate possible storms in an area that involved twenty-five hundred light years of length. Unless their psychologists could unncover the special qualities of his double brain, he might actually accomplish what the Fifty Suns' government wanted. Maltby did not doubt the possibility. He grew aware that Lieutenant Cannons was manipulating the controls of the orbit table.

The lines of light on the surface flickered and shifted. Then settled like the balls in a game of chance. Maltby selected six that ran deep into the great storm. Ten minutes after that he felt the faint jar as the ship began to move. He stood up frowning. Odd that they should act without *some* verification of his—

"This way," said the old man.

Maltby thought sharply: This couldn't be all. Any minute now they'd start on him and—

His thought ended.

He was in space. Far, far below was the receding planet of Kaider III. To one side gleamed the vast dark hull of the battleship; and on every other side, and up, and down, were stars and the distances of dark space. In spite of all his will, the shock was inexpressibly violent.

His active mind jerked. He staggered physically; and he would have fallen like a blindfolded creature except that, in the movement of trying to keep on his feet, he recognized that he *was* still on his feet.

His whole being steadied. Instinctively, he—tilted—his second mind awake, and pushed it forward. Put its more mechanical and precise qualities, its Dellian strength, between his other self and whatever the human beings might be doing against him.

Somewhere in the mist of darkness and blazing stars, a woman's clear and resonant voice said: "Well, Lieutenant Neslor, did the surprise yield any psychological fruits?"

The reply came from a second, an older-sounding woman's voice:

"After three seconds, noble lady, his resistance leaped to I.Q. 900. Which means they've sent us a Dellian. Your excellency, I thought you specifically asked that their representative be not a Dellian."

Maltby said swiftly into the night around him: "You're quite mistaken. I am not a Dellian. And I assure you that I will lower my resistance to zero if you desire. I reacted instinctively to surprise, naturally enough."

There was a click. The illusion of space and stars snapped out of existence. Maltby saw what he had begun to suspect, that he was, had been all the time, in the meteorology room. Nearby stood the old man, a thin smile on his lined face. On a raised dais, partly hidden behind a long instrument board, sat a handsome young woman.

The old man said in a stately voice, "You are in the presence of Grand Captain, the Right Honorable Gloria Cecily, the Lady Laurr of Noble Laurr. Conduct yourself accordingly."

Maltby bowed but said nothing. The grand captain frowned at him, impressed by his appearance. Tall, magnificent-looking body—strong, supremely intelligent face. In a single flash she noted all the characteristics common to the first-class human and—robot.

These people might be more dangerous than she had thought. She said with unnatural sharpness for her: "As you know, we have to question you. We would prefer that you did not take offense. You have told us that Cassidor VII, the chief planet of the Fifty Suns, is twenty-five hundred light years from here. Normally, we would spend many years *feeling* our way across such an immense gap of uncharted star-filled space. But you have given us a choice of orbits. We must make sure those orbits are honest, offered without guile or harmful purpose. To that end we have to ask you to open your mind and answer our questions under the strictest psychological surveillance."

"I have orders," said Maltby, "to cooperate with you in every way."

He had wondered how he would feel, now that the hour of decision was upon him. But there was nothing unnormal. His body was a little stiffer, but his minds—he withdrew his *self* into the background and left his Dellian mind to confront all the questions that came. His Dellian mind that he had deliberately kept apart from his thoughts. That curious mind, which had no will of its own, but which, by remote control, reacted with the full power of an I.Q. of 191.

Sometimes he marveled himself at that second mind of his. It had no creative ability, but its memory was machinelike, and its resistance to outside pressure, as the woman psychologist had so swiftly analyzed, was over nine hundred. To be exact, the equivalent of I.Q. 917.

"What is your name?"

That was the way it began: His name, distinction—he answered everything quietly, positively, without hesitation. When he had finished, when he had sworn to the truth of every word about the storms, there was a long moment of dead silence. And then, a middle-aged woman stepped out of the nearby wall. She motioned him to a chair and when he was seated she tilted his head and began to examine it. She did it gently; her fingers were caressing as a lover's. But when she looked up she said sharply:

"You're not a Dellian or a non-Dellian. And the molecular structure of your brain and body is the most curious I have ever seen. All the molecules are twins. I saw a similar arrangement once in an artificial electronic structure where an attempt was being made to balance an unstable structure. The parallel isn't exact, but mm-m-m, I must try to remember what the end result was of that experiment." She stopped. "What is your explanation? What are you?"

Maltby sighed. He had determined to tell only the one

main lie. Not that it mattered so far as his double brain was concerned. But untruths effected slight variations in blood pressure, created neural spasms and disturbed muscular integration. He couldn't take the risk of even one more than was absolutely necessary. "I'm a Mixed Man," he explained. He described briefly how the cross between the Dellian and non-Dellian, so long impossible, had finally been brought about, a hundred years before. The use of cold and pressure—

"Just a moment," said the psychologist. She disappeared. When she stepped again out of the wall transmitter, she was thoughtful.

"He seems to be telling the truth," she confessed, almost reluctantly.

"What is this?" snapped the grand captain. "Ever since we ran into the first citizen of the Fifty Suns, the psychology department has qualified every statement it issues. I thought Psychology was the only perfect science. Either he is telling the truth or he isn't."

The older woman looked unhappy. She stared very hard at Maltby, seemed baffled by his cool gaze, and finally faced her superior, said: "It's that double molecule structure of his brain. Except for that, I see no reason why you shouldn't order full acceleration."

To herself, Gloria was thinking: "This is it. This is what I've been looking for. There has actually been offspring of a marriage between Dellian and non-Dellian."

She had no clear idea what it might mean. She said aloud with a faint covering smile: "I shall have Captain Maltby to dinner. I'm sure he will co-operate then with any further studies you may be prepared to make at the time. Meanwhile, have someone take him to suitable quarters."

She turned, and spoke into a communicator: "Central Engines, step up to half a light year a minute on the following orbit—"

Maltby listened, estimating. Half a light year a minute. It would take a while to attain that speed, but—in eight hours they'd strike the storm.

In eight hours he'd be having dinner with the grand captain.

Eight hours!

After he had gone, Lady Laurr studied her companion humorlessly. "Well, what do you think?"

"It's hard to believe they would dare trick us at this stage." The psychologist's voice had baffled anger in it.

The grand captain said slowly: "They have quite an intricate system here. The only worthwhile maps are all on planets. The men who know how to interpret the maps are on ships. By use of code words given by people who cannot interpret, the astrogators make their calculations. The only way we can know that Captain Maltby is telling us the truth is by psychological tests. As in the past I am gambling on your skill. Undoubtedly, something is being planned, but we cannot let ourselves be paralyzed by fear. We must assume that any trap we fall into we shall be able to get out by sheer mechanical power, if nothing else. Meanwhile, leave no stone unturned. Keep watching that man. We have still to discover how the *Atmion* escaped from us."

"I'll do my best," said the older woman harshly.

Chapter Eleven

THE full flood of a contraterrene Nova impinging upon terrene gases already infuriated by seetee gone insane—that was the new greater storm.

The exploding giant sun added weight to the diffuse, maddened thing. And it added something far more deadly. Speed! From peak to peak of velocity the tumult of ultrafire leaped. The swifter crags of the storm danced and burned with an absolutely hellish fury. The sequence of action was rapid almost beyond the bearance of matter. First raced the light of the Nova, blazing its warning at more than a hundred and eighty-six thousand miles a second to all who knew that it flashed from the edge of an interstellar storm.

But the advance glare of warning was nullified by the colossal speed of the storm. For weeks and months it drove through the vast night at a velocity that was only a bare measure short of that of light itself.

The dinner dishes had been cleared away. Maltby was thinking: In half an hour—*half an hour!*

He was wondering shakily just what did happen to a battleship suddenly confronted with thousands of gravities of deceleration. Aloud he was saying: "My day? I spent it in the library. I was interested in the recent history of Earth's interstellar colonization. I'm curious as to what is done with groups like the Mixed Men. I mentioned to you that, after the war in which they were defeated, largely because there were so few of them, the Mixed Men hid themselves from the Fifty Suns. I was one of the captured children who—"

There was an interruption; a cry from the wall communicator: *"Noble lady, I've solved it!*

A moment fled before Maltby recognized the strained voice of the woman psychologist. He had almost forgotten that she was supposed to be studying him. Her next words chilled him.

"Two minds! I thought of it a little while ago and rigged up a twin watching device. Ask him—*ask* him the question about the storms. Meanwhile stop the ship. At once!"

Maltby's dark gaze clashed hard with the steely, narrowed eyes of the grand captain. Without hesitation he concentrated his two minds on her, forced her to say:

"Don't be silly, lieutenant. One person can't have two brains. Explain yourself further."

His hope was delay. They had ten minutes in which they could save themselves. He must waste every second of that time, resist all their efforts, try to control the situation. If only his special, three-dimensional hypnotism worked through communicators—

It didn't. Lines of light leaped at him from the wall and crisscrossed his body, held him in his chair like so many unbreakable cables. Even as he was bound hand and foot by the palpable energy, a second complex of forces built up before his face, barred his thought pressure from the grand captain, and finally coned over his head like a dunce cap.

He was caught as neatly as if a dozen men had swarmed with their strength and weight over his body. Maltby relaxed and laughed. "Too late," he taunted. "It'll take at least an hour for this ship to reduce to a safe speed; and at this velocity you can't turn aside in time to avoid the greatest storm in this part of the universe."

That wasn't strictly true. There was still time and room to sheer off before the advancing storm in any of the fronting directions. The impossibility was to turn toward the storm's tail, or its great bulging sides.

His thought was interrupted by the first cry from the young woman; a piercing cry; "Central engines! Reduce speed! Emergency!"

There was a jar that shook the walls and a pressure that tore at his muscles. Maltby adjusted and then stared across the table at the grand captain. She was smiling, a frozen mask of a smile, and she said from between clenched teeth: "Lieutenant Neslor, use any means physical or otherwise, but make him talk. There must be something."

"His second mind is the key," the psychologist's voice came. "It's not Dellian. It has only normal resistance. I shall subject it to the greatest concentration of conditioning ever focused on a human brain, using the two basics: sex and logic. I shall have to use you, noble lady, as the object of his affections."

"Hurry!" said the young woman. Her voice was like a metal bar.

Maltby sat in a mist, mental and physical. Deep in his mind was awareness that he was an entity, and that irresistible machines were striving to mold his thought. He resisted. The resistance was as strong as his life, as intense as all the billions and quadrillions of impulses that had shaped his being, could make it.

But the outside thought, the pressure, grew stronger. How silly of him to resist Earth—when this lovely woman of Earth loved him, loved him, loved him. Glorious was that civilization of Earth and the main galaxy. Three hundred million billion people. The very first contact would rejuvenate the Fifty Suns. How lovely she is; I must save her. She means everything to me.

As from a great distance, he began to hear his own voice, explaining what must be done, just how the ship must be turned, in what direction, how much time there was. He tried to stop himself, but inexorably his voice went on, mouthing the words that spelled a second defeat for the Fifty Suns.

The mist began to fade. The terrible pressure eased from his straining mind. The damning stream of words ceased to pour from his lips. He sat up shakily, conscious that the energy cords and the energy cap had been withdrawn from his body. He heard the grand captain say into a communicator:

"By making a point 0100 turn we shall miss the storm by seven light weeks. I admit it is an appallingly sharp curve, but I feel that we should have at least that much leeway."

She turned and stared at Maltby: "Prepare yourself. At half a light year a minute even a hundredth of a degree turn makes some people black out."

"Not me," said Maltby, and tensed his Dellian muscles.

She fainted three times during the next four minutes as he sat there watching her. But each time she recovered within seconds. "We human beings," she said wanly, "are a poor lot. But at least we know how to endure."

The terrible minutes dragged. And dragged. Maltby began to feel the strain of that infinitesimal turn. He thought at last: How could these people ever hope to survive a direct hit on a storm?

Abruptly it was over; a man's voice said quietly:

"We have followed the prescribed course, noble lady, and are now out of dang—"

He broke off with a shout: "Captain, the light of a Nova sun has just flashed from the direction of the storm!"

Chapter Twelve

IN THOSE minutes before disaster struck, the battleship *Star Cluster* glowed like an immense and brilliant jewel. The warning glare from the Nova set off an incredible roar of emergency clamor through all of her hundred and twenty decks. From end to end her lights flicked on. They burned row by row straight across her four thousand feet of length with the hard twinkle of cut gems. In the reflection of that light, the black mountain that was her hull looked like the fabulous planet of Cassidor, her destination, as seen at night from a far darkness, sown with diamond shining cities.

Silent as a ghost, grand and wonderful beyond all imagination, glorious in her power, the great ship slid through the blackness along the special river of time and space which was her plotted course.

Even as she rode into the storm there was nothing visible. The space ahead looked as clear as any vacuum. So tenuous were the gases that made up the storm that the ship would not even have been aware of them if it had been traveling at atomic speeds. Violent the disintegration of matter in that storm might be, and the sole source of cosmic rays the hardest energy in the known universe. But the immense, the cataclysmic danger to the *Star Cluster* was a direct result of her own terrible velocity.

Striking that mass of gas at half a light year a minute was like running into an unending solid wall. The great ship shuddered in every plate as the deceleration tore at her gigantic strength. In seconds she had run the gamut of all the recoil systems her designers had planned for her as a unit.

She began to break up.

And still everything was according to the original purpose of the superb engineering firm that had built her. The limit of unit strain reached, she dissolved into her nine thousand separate sections.

Streamlined needles of metal were those sections, four hundred feet long, forty feet wide; silverlike shapes sinuated cunningly through the gases, letting the pressure of them slide off their smooth sides. But it wasn't enough. Metal groaned from the torture of deceleration. In the deceleration chambers, men and women lay at the bare edge of consciousness, enduring agony that seemed beyond endurance. Hundreds of sections careened through space avoiding each other by means of automatic screens.

And still, in spite of the hideously maintained velocity, that mass of gases was not bridged; light years of thickness still had to be covered.

Once more all the limits of human strength was reached. The final action was chemical, directly on the thirty thousand human bodies—those bodies for whose sole benefit all the marvelous safety devices had been conceived and constructed, the poor, fragile, human beings who through all the ages had persisted in dying under normal conditions from a pressure of something less than fifteen gravities.

The prompt reaction of the automatics in rolling back every floor, and plunging every person into the deceleration chambers of each section—that saving reaction was abruptly augmented as the deceleration chamber was flooded by a special type of gas.

Wet was that gas, and clinging. It settled thickly on the clothes of the humans, soaked through to the skin and *through* the skin, into every part of the body.

Sleep came gently, and with it a wonderful relaxation. The blood grew immune to shock; muscles that, a minute before, had been drawn with anguish—loosened; the brain impregnated with life-giving chemicals that relieved it of all shortages remained untroubled even by dreams. Everyone grew enormously flexible to gravitation pressures—a hundred—a hundred and fifty gravities of deceleration; and still the life force clung.

The great heart of the Universe beat on. The storm roared along its inescapable artery, creating the radiance of life, purging the dark of its poisons—and at last the tiny ships in their separate courses burst its great bounds.

They began to come together, to seek each other, as if among them there was an irresistible passion that demanded intimacy of union. Automatically they slid into their old positions; the battleship *Star Cluster* began again to take form—but there were gaps. Segments were lost.

On the third day, Acting Grand Captain Rutgers called the surviving captains to the forward bridge, where he was temporarily making his headquarters. After the conference a communique was issued to the crew:

At 008 hours this morning a message was received from Grand Captain, the Right Honorable Gloria Cecily, the Lady Laurr of Noble Laurr, I.C., C.M., G.K.R. She has been forced down on a planet of a yellow-white sun. Her ship crashed on landing, and is unrepairable. As all communication with her has been by non-directional subspace radio, and as it will be utterly impossible to locate such an ordinary type sun among so many millions of other suns, the Captains in session regret to report that our noble lady's name must now be added to that longest of all lists of naval casualties: the list of those who have been lost forever on active duty.

The admiralty lights will burn blue until further notice.

Chapter Thirteen

HER back was to him as he approached. Maltby hesitated, then tensed his mind, and held her there beside the section of the ship that had been the main bridge of the *Star Cluster*.

The long metal shape lay half buried in the marshy ground of the great valley, its lower end jutting down into the shimmering, deep, yellowish black waters of the sluggish river. He paused a few feet from the tall, slim woman, and, still holding her unaware of him, examined once again the environment that was to be their life. The fine spray of dark rain that had dogged his exploration walk was retreating over the yellow rim of valley to the "west." As he watched, a small yellow sun burst out from behind a curtain of dark, ocherous clouds and glared at him brilliantly. Below was an expanse of jungle that glinted strangely brown and yellow. Everywhere was that dark-brown and intense, almost liquid yellow.

Maltby sighed—and turned his attention to the woman, willed her not to see him as he walked around in front of her. He had given a great deal of thought to the Right Honorable Gloria Cecily during his walk. Basically, of course, the problem of a man and a woman who were destined to live the rest of their lives together, alone on a remote planet, was very simple. Particularly in view of the fact that one of the two had been conditioned to be in love with the other. He smiled grimly. He could appreciate the artificial origin of that love, but that didn't dispose of the profound fact of it.

The conditioning machine had struck to his very core. Unfortunately, it had not touched her at all; and two days of being alone with her had brought out one reality: The Lady Laurr of Noble Laurr was not even remotely thinking of yielding herself to the normal requirements of the situation. It was time that she was made aware, not because an early solution was necessary, or even desirable, but because she had to realize that the problem existed. He stepped forward and took her in his arms.

She was a tall graceful woman; she fitted into his embrace as if she belonged there; and, because his control of her made her return the kiss, its warmth had an effect beyond his intention. He had intended to free her mind in the middle of the kiss.

He didn't.

When he finally released her, it was only a physical release. Her mind was still completely under his domination. There was a metal chair that had been set just outside one of the doors. He walked over, sank into it and stared up at the grand captain. He felt shaken. The flame of desire that had leaped through him was a telling tribute to the conditioning he had undergone. But it was entirely beyond his previous analysis of the intensity of his own feelings. He had thought he was in full control of himself, and he wasn't. Somehow, the sardonicism, the half detachment, the objectivity, which he had fancied was the keynote of his own reaction to this situation, didn't apply at all. The conditioning machine had been thorough.

He loved this woman with such a violence that the mere touch of her was enough to disconnect his will from operations immediately following. His heart grew quieter as he studied her with a semblance of detachment. She was lovely in a handsome fashion; though almost all robot women of the Dellian race were better looking. Her lips, while medium full, were somehow a trifle cruel; and there was a quality in her eyes that accentuated that cruelty. There were built-up emotions in this woman that would not surrender easily to the necessity of being marooned for life on an unknown planet. It was something he'd have to think over. Until then—

Maltby sighed, and released her from the three dimensional hypnotic spell that his two minds had imposed on her. He had taken the precaution of turning her away from him. He watched her curiously as she stood, back to him, for a moment very still. Then she walked over to a little knob of trees above the springy, soggy marsh land. She climbed this elevation and gazed in the direction from which he had come a few minutes before. She was evidently looking for him. She turned, finally, shading her eyes against the brightness of the sinking yellow sun; came down from the hillock and saw him.

She stopped; her eyes narrowed. She walked over slowly and said with an odd edge on her voice: "You came very quietly. You must have circled and walked in from the west."

"No," he said deliberately. "I stayed in the east."

She seemed to consider that as she regarded him with a slight frown. She pressed her lips together, finally; there was a bruise there that must have hurt, for she winced, then she said:

"What did you discover? Did you find any—"

She stopped. Consciousness of the bruise on her lip must have penetrated at that moment. As her fingers touched the tender spot her eyes came alive with the violence of her comprehension. Before she could speak he said: "Yes, you're quite right."

She stood looking at him; tense with suppressed anger. Finally she relaxed and said in a stony voice: "If you try that again I shall feel justified in shooting you."

Maltby shook his head, unsmiling. "And spend the rest of your life here alone? You'd go mad."

He saw instantly that her basic anger was too great for that kind of logic. He added swiftly: "Besides, you'd have to shoot me in the back. I have no doubt you could do that in the line of duty. But not enough for personal reasons."

To his amazement there were tears in her eyes. Anger tears, obviously. But tears! She stepped forward quickly and slapped his face. "You *robot!*" she sobbed.

He stared at her ruefully; then he laughed and said, with a trace of mockery: "If I remember rightly, the lady who just spoke is the same one who delivered a ringing radio address to all the planets of the Fifty Suns, swearing that in fifteen thousand years, Earth people had forgotten all their prejudices against robots. Is it possible," he finished, "that the problem on *closer* investigation is proving more difficult?"

There was no answer. The Honorable Gloria Cecily brushed past him and disappeared into the interior of the ship. She came out again a few minutes later, her expression serene, and he saw that she had removed all trace of the tears. Her voice was calm as she asked: "What did you discover when you were out? I've been delaying my call to the ship until you returned."

Maltby said: "I thought they asked you to call at 010 hours."

The woman shrugged; and there was a note of arrogance in her voice as she replied:

"They'll take my calls when I make them. Did you find any sign of intelligent life?"

He allowed himself brief pity for a human being who had as many shocks still to absorb as had Grand Captain Laurr. He said finally: "Mostly marsh land in the valley and there's jungle, very old. Even some of the trees are immense, though sections showed no growth rings—some interesting beasts and a four legged, two armed thing that watched me from a distance. It carried a spear but it was too far away for me to use hypnotism on it. There must be a village somewhere near. Perhaps on the valley rim. My idea is that during the next few months I'll cut the ship into small sections and transport it to drier ground. I would say that we have the following information to offer the ship's scientists. We're on a planet of a G-type sun. The sun must be larger than the average yellow-white type and have a larger surface temperature. It must be larger and hotter because, though it's far away, it is hot enough to keep the northern hemisphere of this planet in a semi-tropical condition. The sun was quite a bit north at mid-day, but now it is swinging back to the south. I'd say off-hand that the planet must be tilted about forty degrees, which means there's a cold winter coming up, though that doesn't fit with the age and type of vegetation."

The lady Laurr was frowning. "It doesn't seem very helpful," she said. "But of course, I'm only an executive."

"And I'm only a meteorologist."

"Exactly. Come in. Perhaps my astrophysicist can make something of it."

"*Your* astrophysicist!" said Maltby. But he didn't say it aloud. He followed her into the segment of the ship and closed the door.

He examined the interior of the main bridge with a wry smile as she seated herself before the astroplate. The very imposing glitter of the instrument board that occupied one entire wall was ironical now. All the machinery it had controlled was far away in space. Once it had dominated the entire Greater Magellanic Cloud; now his own hand gun was a more potent instrument. He grew aware that Lady Laurr was looking up at him.

"I don't understand it," she said. "They don't answer."

"Perhaps"—Maltby could not keep the faint sadonicism out of his tone—"perhaps they may really have had a good reason for wanting you to call at 010 hours."

She made a faint exasperated movement with her facial muscles but did not answer. Maltby went on coolly: "After all, it doesn't matter. They're only going through routine motions, the idea being to leave no loophole of rescue unlooked for. I can't even imagine the kind of miracle it would take for anybody to find us."

The woman seemed not to have heard. She frowned and said: "How is it that we've never heard a Fifty Suns broadcast? I intended to ask about that before. Not once during our ten years in the Cloud did we catch so much as a whisper of radio energy."

Maltby shrugged. "All radios operate on an extremely complicated variable wave length—changes every twentieth of a second. Your instruments would register a tick once every ten minutes, and—"

He was cut off by a voice from the astroplate. A man's face was there—Acting Grand Captain Rutgers.

"Oh there you are captain," the woman said. "What kept you?"

"We're in the process of landing our forces on Cassidor VII," was the reply. "As you know, regulations require that the grand captain—"

"Oh yes. Are you free now?"

"No. I've taken a moment to see that everything is right with you, and then I'll switch you over to Captain Planston."

"How is the landing proceeding?"

"Perfectly. We have made contact with the government. They seem resigned. But now I must leave. Goodby, my lady."

His face flickered and was gone. The plate went blank. It was about as curt a greeting as anybody had ever received. But Maltby, sunk in his own gloom, scarcely noticed.

So it was all over. The desperate scheming of the Fifty Suns leaders, his own attempt to destroy the great battleship, proved futile against an invincible foe. For a moment he felt very close to the defeat, with all its implications. Consciousness came finally that the fight no longer mattered in his life. But the knowledge failed to shake his dark mood.

He saw that the Right Honorable Gloria Cecily had an expression of mixed elation and annoyance on her fine, strong face; and there was no doubt that she didn't *feel*—disconnected—from the mighty events out there in space. Nor had she missed the implications of the abruptness of the interview.

The astroplate grew bright again and a face appeared on it—one that Maltby hadn't seen before. It was a heavyjowled oldish man with a ponderous voice that said: "Privilege, your ladyship—hope we can find something that will enable us to make a rescue. Never give up hope, I say, until the last nail's driven in your coffin."

He chuckled; and the woman said: "Captain Maltby will give you all the information he has, then no doubt you can give him some advice, Captain Planston. Neither he nor I, unfortunately, are astrophysicists."

"Can't be experts on every subject," Captain Planston puffed. "Er, Captain Maltby, what do you know?"

Maltby gave him his information briefly, then waited while the other gave instructions. There wasn't much:

"Find out length of seasons. Interested in that yellow effect of the sunlight and the deep brown. Take the following photographs, using ortho-sensitive film—use three dyes, a red sensitive, a blue and a yellow. Take a spectrum reading—what I want to check on is that maybe you've got a strong blue sun there, with the ultraviolet barred by the heavy atmosphere, and all the heat and light coming in on the yellow band. I'm not offering much hope, mind you—the Greater Cloud is packed with blue suns—five hundred thousand of them brighter than Sirius.

"Finally, get that season information from the natives. Make a point of it. Good-by!"

Chapter Fourteen

THE native was wary. He persisted in retreating elusively
into the jungle; and his four legs gave him a speed advantage of which he seemed to be aware. For he kept
coming back, tantalizingly. The woman watched with
amusement, then exasperation.

"Perhaps," she suggested, "if we separated, and I drove
him toward you?"

She saw the frown on his face as Maltby nodded reluctantly. His voice was strong, tense. "He's leading us
into an ambush. Turn on the sensitives in your helmet and
carry your gun. Don't be too hasty about firing, but don't
hesitate in a crisis. A spear can make an ugly wound; and
we haven't got the best facilities for handling anything
like that."

His orders caused her momentary irritation. He seemed
not to be aware that she was as conscious as he of the
requirements of the situation. The Right Honorable
Gloria sighed. If they had to stay on this planet, there
would have to be some major psychological adjustments,
and not—she thought grimly—only by herself.

"*Now!*" said Maltby beside her, swiftly. "Notice the
way the ravine splits in two. I came this far yesterday and
they join about two hundred yards farther on. He's gone
up the left fork, I'll take the right. You stop here, let him
come back to see what's happened, then drive him on."

Maltby was gone, like a shadow, along a dark path that
wound under thick foliage. Silence settled.

She waited. After a minute she felt herself alone in a
yellow and black world that had been lifeless since time

began. She thought: This was what Maltby meant yesterday when he'd said she wouldn't dare shoot him—and remain alone. It hadn't penetrated then. It did now. Alone, on a nameless planet of a mediocre sun, one woman waking up every morning on a moldering ship that rested its unliving metal shape on a dark, muggy, yellow marsh land.

She stood somber. There was no doubt that the problem of Dellian and Mixed Man, and human being would have to be solved here as well as out there.

A sound pulled her out of her gloom. As she watched, abruptly more alert, a catlike head peered cautiously from a line of bushes a hundred yards away across the clearing. It was an interesting head. Its ferocity was not the least of its fascinating qualities. The yellowish body was invisible now in the underbrush, but she had caught enough glimpses of it earlier to recognize that it was the CC type, of the almost universal Centaur family. Its body was evenly balanced between its hind and forelegs.

It watched her and its great glistening black eyes were round with puzzlement. Its head twisted from side to side, obviously searching for Maltby. She waved her gun and walked forward. Instantly the creature disappeared. She could hear it with her sensitives, running into distance. Abruptly it slowed; then there was no sound at all.

"He's got it," she thought.

She felt impressed. These two-brained Mixed Men, she thought, were bold and capable. It would really be too bad if prejudice prevented them from being absorbed into the galactic civilization of Imperial Earth. She watched him a few minutes later, using the block system of communication with the creature. Maltby looked up, saw her. He shook his head as if puzzled.

"He says it's always been warm like this, and that he's been alive for thirteen hundred moons. And that a moon is forty suns—forty days. He wants us to come up a little further along this valley, but that's too transparent for comfort. Our move is to make a cautious friendly gesture, and—"

He stopped short. Before she could even realize anything was wrong, her mind was caught, her muscles galvanized. She was thrown sideways and downward so fast that the blow of striking the ground was pure agony.

She lay there stunned, and out of the corner of her eye she saw the spear plunge through the air where she had been. She twisted, rolled over—her own free will now—and jerked her gun in the direction from which the spear had come. There was a second centaur there, racing away along a bare slope. Her finger pressed on the control; and then—

"Don't!" It was Maltby, his voice low: "It was a scout the others sent ahead to see what was happening. He's done his work. It's all over."

She lowered her gun and saw with annoyance that her hand was shaking, her whole body trembling. She parted her lips to say: "Thanks for saving my life!" Then she closed them again. Because the words would have quavered. And because— Saved her life! Her mind poised on the edge of blankness with the shock of the thought. Incredibly she had never before been in personal danger from an individual creature. There had been the time when her battleship had run into the outer fringes of a sun; and there was the cataclysm of the storm just past. But these had been impersonal menaces to be met with technical virtuosities and the hard training of the service. This was different.

All the way back to the segment of the ship she tried to fathom what the difference meant. It seemed to her finally that she had it.

"Spectrum featureless." Maltby gave his findings over the astro. "No dark lines at all; two of the yellow bands so intense that they hurt my eyes. As you suggested, apparently what we have here is a blue sun whose strong violet radiation is cut off by the atmosphere.

"However," he finished, "the uniqueness of that effect is confined to our planet here, a derivation of the thick atmosphere. Any questions?"

"No-o!" The astrophysicist looked thoughtful. "And I can give you no further instructions. I'll have to examine this material. Will you ask Lady Laurr to come in? I'd like to speak to her privately if you please."

"Of course."

When she had come, Maltby went outside and watched the moon come up. Darkness—he had noticed it the previous night—brought a vague, overall violet haze. Explained now!

An eighty-degree temperature on a planet that, the angular diameter of the sun being what it was, would have been minus one hundred eighty degrees, if the sun's apparent color had been real. A blue sun, one of the five hundred thousand— Interesting but— Maltby smiled savagely. Captain Planston's "No further instructions!" had a finality about it that—

He shivered involuntarily. And after a moment tried to picture himself sitting like this, a year hence, staring up at an unchanged moon. Ten years, twenty—

He grew aware that the woman had come to the doorway and was gazing at him where he sat on the chair. He looked up. The stream of white light from inside the ship caught the queer expression on her face, gave her a strange bleached look after the yellowness that had seemed a part of her complexion all day.

"We shall receive no more astro-radio calls," she said and, turning, went inside.

Maltby nodded to himself, almost idly. It was hard and brutal, this abrupt cutting off of communication. But the regulations governing such situations were precise. The marooned ones must realize with utter clarity without false hopes and without curious illusions produced by radio communications, that they were cut off forever. Forever on their own.

Well, so be it. A fact was a fact, to be faced with resolution. There had been a chapter on castaways in one of the books he had read on the battleship. It had stated that nine hundred million human beings had, during recorded history, been marooned on then undiscovered planets. Most of these planets had eventually been found; and on no less than ten thousand of them, great populations had sprung up from the original nucleus of castaways. The law prescribed that a castaway could not withhold himself or herself from participating in such population increases—regardless of previous rank. Castaways must forget considerations of sensitivity and individualism, and think of themselves as instruments of race expansion. There were penalties; naturally inapplicable if no rescue was effected, but ruthlessly applied whenever recalcitrants were found.

Conceivably the courts might determine that a human being and a—well—robot constituted a special case. Half an hour must have passed while he sat there. He stood up finally, conscious of hunger. He had forgotten all about supper. He felt a qualm of self-annoyance. Damn it, this was not the night to appear to be putting pressure on her. Sooner or later she would have to be convinced that she ought to do her share of the cooking.

But not tonight.

He hurried inside, toward the compact kitchen that was part of every segment of the ship. In the corridor, he paused. A blaze of light streamed from the kitchen door. Somebody was whistling softly and tunelessly but cheerfully; and there was an odor of cooking vegetables, and hot *lak* meat.

They almost bumped in the doorway. "I was just going to call you," she said.

The meal was silent and quickly over. They put the dishes into the automatic and went and sat in the great lounge. Maltby saw finally that the woman was studying him with amused eyes.

"Is there any possibility," she said abruptly, "that a Mixed Man and a human woman can have children?"

"Frankly," Maltby confessed, "I doubt it."

He launched into a description of the cold and pressure process that had molded the protoplasm to make the original Mixed Men. When he finished he saw that her eyes were still regarding him with a faint amusement. She said in an odd tone: "A very curious thing happened to me today, after that native threw his spear. I realized," she seemed for a moment to have difficulty in speaking— "I realized that I had, so far as I was personally concerned, solved the robot problem. Naturally," she finished quietly, "I would not have withheld myself in any event. But it is pleasant to know that I like you without"—she smiled—"qualifications."

Chapter Fifteen

BLUE sun that looked yellow. Maltby sat in a chair the following morning puzzling over it. He half expected a visit from the natives, and so he was determined to stay near the ship that day. He kept his eyes aware of the clearing edges, the valley rims, the jungle trails, but—

There was a law, he remembered, that governed the shifting of light to other wave bands, to yellow for instance. Rather complicated, but in view of the fact that all instruments of the main bridge were controls of instruments, not the machines themselves, he'd have to depend on mathematics if he ever hoped to visualize the kind of sun that was out there. Most of the heat probably came through the ultraviolet range. But that was uncheckable. So leave it alone and stick to the yellow.

He went into the ship. Gloria was nowhere in sight, but her bedroom door was closed. He found a notebook, returned to his chair and began to figure. An hour later he stared at the answer: One million three hundred thousand million miles. About a fifth of a light year. He laughed curtly. That was that. He'd have to get better data than he had or—

Or would he?

His mind poised. In a single flash of understanding, the stupendous truth burst upon him. With a cry he leaped to his feet. He was whirling to race through the door as a long, black shadow slid across him. The shadow was so vast, instantly darkening the whole valley, that involuntarily, Maltby halted, and looked up.

The battleship *Star Cluster* hung low over the yellow-brown jungle planet, already disgorging a lifeboat that

114

glinted a yellowish silver as it circled out into the sunlight, and started down. Maltby had only a moment with the woman before the lifeboat landed. "To think," he said, "that I just now figured out the truth."

She was, he saw, not looking at him. Her gaze seemed far away. He went on: "As for the rest, the best method, I imagine, is to put me in the conditioning chamber, and—"

Still without looking at him, she cut him off: "Don't be ridiculous. You must not imagine that I feel embarrassed because you have kissed me. I shall receive you in my quarters later."

A bath, new clothes—at last Maltby stepped through the transmitter into the astrophysics department. His own first realization of the tremendous truth, while generally accurate, had lacked detailed facts.

"Ah, Maltby!" The chief of the department came forward and shook hands. "Some sun you picked there—we suspected from your first description of the yellowness and the black. But naturally we couldn't rouse your hopes— Forbidden, you know. The axial tilt, the apparent length of a summer in which jungle trees of great size showed no growth rings—very suggestive. The featureless spectrum with its complete lack of dark lines—almost conclusive. Final proof was that the ortho-sensitive film was overexposed, while the blue and red sensitives were badly underexposed. This star-type is so immensely hot that practically all of its energy radiation is far in the ultravisible. A secondary radiation—a sort of fluorescence in the star's own atmosphere—produces the visible yellow when a minute fraction of the appalling ultraviolet radiation is transformed into longer wave lengths by helium atoms. A fluorescent lamp, in a fashion—but on a scale that is more than ordinarily cosmic in its violence. The total radiation reaching the planet was naturally tremendous; the surface radiation, after passing through miles of absorbing ozone, water vapor, carbon dioxide and other gases, was very different. No wonder the native said it has always been hot. The summer lasts four thousand years. The normal radiation of that appalling star type—

the aeon-in-aeon-out radiation rate—is about equal to a full-fledged Nova at its catastrophic maximum of violence. It has a period of a few hours, and is equivalent to approximately a hundred million ordinary suns. Nova O, we call that brightest of all stars; and there's only one in the Greater Magellanic Cloud, the great and glorious S Doradus. When I asked you to call Grand Captain Laurr, and I told her that out of a hundred million suns she had picked—"

It was at that point that Maltby cut him off: "Just a minute," he said, "did you say you told Lady Laurr *last night?*"

"Was it night down there?" Captain Planston was interested. "Well, well— By the way, I almost forgot—this marrying and giving in marriage is not so important to me now that I am an old man. But congratulations."

The conversation was too swift for Maltby. His minds were still examining the first statement. That she had known all the time. He came up, groping, before the new words. "Congratulations?" he echoed.

"Definitely time she had a husband," boomed the captain. "She's been a career woman, you know. Besides, it'll have a revivifying effect on other robots . . . pardon me. Assure you, the name means nothing to me. Anyway, Lady Laurr herself made the announcement a few minutes ago, so come down and see me again." He turned away with a wave of a thick hand.

Maltby headed for the nearest transmitter. She would probably be expecting him by now.

She would not be disappointed.

Chapter Sixteen

THE globe was palely luminous, and about three feet in diameter. It hung in the air at approximately the center of the room, and its lowest arc was at the level of Maltby's chin. Frowning, his double mind tensed, he climbed out of the bed, put on his slippers, and walked slowly around the light-shape. As he stepped past it, it vanished.

He twisted hastily back—and there it was again. Maltby allowed himself a grim smile. It was as he had thought, a projection, pointing out of sub-space at his bed, and having no material existence in his room. Therefore it couldn't be seen from the rear. His frown deepened with gathering puzzlement. If he didn't know that *they* did not possess such a communicator, he'd guess that he was about to be advised that the time had come for action.

He hoped not, fervently. He was as far as ever from a decision. Yet who else would be trying to reach him? The impulse came to touch the button that would connect the control center of the big spaceship with what was going on in his room. It wouldn't do to have Gloria think that he was in secret communication with outsiders. If she ever got suspicious, even the fact that he was married to her wouldn't save his two minds from being investigated by the ship's psychologist, Lieutenant Neslor.

However, he had other commitments than marriage. He sat down on the bed, scowled at the thing and said: "I'm going to make an assumption as to your identity. What do you want?"

A voice, a very strong, confident voice spoke *through* the globe. "You think you know who is calling in spite of the unusual means?"

117

Maltby recognized the voice. His eyes narrowed, he swallowed hard; then he had control of himself. He remembered that there might be other listeners, who would draw conclusions from his instant recognition of a voice. It was for them that he said, "The logic of it is comparatively simple. I am a Mixed Man aboard the Earth battleship *Star Cluster*, which is cruising in the Fifty Suns region of the Greater Magellanic Cloud. Who would be trying to get in touch with me but the Hidden Ones of my own race?"

"Knowing this," said the voice pointedly, "you have nevertheless made no attempt to betray us?"

Maltby was silent. He wasn't sure he liked that remark. Like his own words, he recognized that these were aimed at possible listeners. But it was not a friendly act to call the attention of those listeners to the fact that he *was* keeping this conversation to himself. More sharply than before it struck him that he had better remember his political situation, both here on the ship, and out there. And weigh every word as he uttered it. He stared at the light-thing and decided that he'd better bring the identity of the man beyond into the open. He said curtly: "Who are you?"

"Hunston!"

"Oh!" said Maltby. His surprise was not altogether simulated. There was a difference between an inward recognition of a voice, and having that recognition verbally verified. The implications of the identity somehow sank in deeper.

Hunston had been released after the *Star Cluster* had located the Fifty Suns. Since then, Maltby—because of his own situation—had had virtually no communication with the outside world. Softly, Maltby repeated an earlier question: "What do you want?"

"Your diplomatic support."

Maltby said, "My what?"

The voice grew resonant and proud. "In accordance with our belief, which you must surely share, that the Mixed Men are entitled to an equal part in the government of the Fifty Suns, regardless of the smallness of their numbers, I have today ordered that control be seized of every planet in the system. At this moment, the armies of the Mixed Men, backed by the greatest assembly of super-weapons known in any galaxy, are carrying out landing operations, and will shortly attain control. You—" the voice paused; then quietly, "You are following me, Captain Maltby?"

The question was like the silence after a clap of thunder. Slowly, Maltby emerged from the hard shock of the news. He climbed to his feet, then sank back again. Consciousness came finally that, though the world had changed, the room was still there. The room, the light-globe and himself.

Anger came then like a leaping fire. Savagely he snapped: "*You* gave this order—" He caught himself. His brain geared to lightning comprehension, he examined the implications of the information. At last, with a bleak realization that in his position he could not argue the matter, he said, "You're depending on acceptance of a *fait accompli*. What I know of the unalterable policies of Imperial Earth, convinces me your hope is vain."

"On the contrary," came the quick reply. "Only Grand Captain, the Lady Laurr must be persuaded. She has full authority to act as she sees fit. And she is your wife."

Cooler now, Maltby hesitated. It was interesting that Hunston, having acted on his own, was now seeking his support. Not too interesting though. What really held Maltby silent was the sudden realization that he had *known* something like this would happen—had known it from the very instant the news had been flashed that an Earth battleship had discovered the civilization of the Fifty Suns, months ago now. Ten years, five years, even one year hence, the seal of Earth's approval would be set forever on the Fifty Suns democratic system *as it was*. And the laws of that government expressly excluded the Mixed Men from any participation whatsoever. At this moment, this month, a change was still theoretically possible. After that—

It was clear that he personally had been too slow in making up his mind. The passions of other men had surged to thoughts of action, and finally to action itself. He would have to leave the ship somehow, and find out what was going on. For the moment, however, caution was the word.

Maltby said, "I'm not averse to presenting your arguments to my wife. But some of your statements do not impress me in the slightest. You have said 'the greatest assembly of super-weapons in any galaxy.' I admit that this method of using sub-space radio is new to me, but your statement as a whole must be nonsense. You cannot possibly know the weapons possessed by even this one battleship because, in spite of all my opportunity, I don't know. It is a safe assumption, furthermore, that no one ship can carry some of the larger weapons that Earth could muster at short notice anywhere in the charted universe. You cannot, isolated as we have all been, so much as guess what these weapons are, let alone declare with certainty that yours are better. Therefore, my question in that connection is this: why do you even mention such an implied threat? Of all your arguments, it is the least likely to rouse any enthusiasm for your cause. Well?"

On the main bridge of the big ship, the Right Honorable Gloria Cecily turned from the viewing plate, which showed Maltby's room. Her fine face was crinkled with thought. She said slowly to the other woman: "What do you make of it, Lieutenant Neslor?"

The ship's psychologist replied steadily: "I think, noble lady, this is the moment we discussed when you first asked me what would be the psychological effects of your marriage to Peter Maltby."

The grand captain stared at her subordinate in astonishment. "Are you mad? His reaction has been correct in every detail. He has told me at great length his opinions of the situation in the Fifty Suns; and every word fits—"

There was a soft buzz from the intership radio. A man's head and shoulders came onto the plate.

"Draydon," he said, "Commander of Communications speaking. In reference to your question about the ultrawave radio now focused in your husband's bedroom, a

similar device was invented in the main galaxy about a
hundred and ninety years ago. The intention was to
install it in all new warships, and in all the older ships
above cruiser class, but we were on our way before mass
production began.

"In this field at least, therefore, the Mixed Men have
equaled the inventions of human creative genius, though
it is difficult to know how so few could accomplish so
much. The very smallness of their numbers make it highly
probable that they are not aware that our finders would
instantly report the presence of their energy manifesta-
tion. They cannot possibly have discovered all the by-
products of their invention. Any questions, noble lady?"

"Yes, how does it work?"

"Power. Sheer, unadulterated power. The ultra-waves
are directed in a great cone toward a wide sector of space
in which the receiver ship is believed to be. Every engine
in the sending ship is geared to the ray. I believe that
experimentally, contact was established over distances as
great as thirty-five hundred light-years."

"Yes," the Lady Laurr was impatient, "but what is the
principle? How, for instance, would they pick out the
Star Cluster from a hundred other ships?"

"As you know," came the reply, "our ship constantly
emits identification rays on a special wave length. The
ultra rays are tuned to that wave length, and when they
contact, react literally instantaneously. Immediately, all
the rays focus on the center of the source of the identification waves, and remain focused regardless of speed
or change of direction. Naturally, once the carrier wave
is focused, sending picture and voice beams over it is
simple."

"I see." She looked thoughtful. "Thank you."

She clicked off the connection and turned again to the
image of the scene in Maltby's room.

"Very well," her husband said, "I shall present your
arguments to my wife."

The answer of the light-globe was: it vanished. She
sat cold. The whole interview had been registered on
a beam, so the part she'd missed could be run off again

later. She turned slowly to Lieutenant Neslor, and expressed the thought that hadn't left her mind for an instant: "What are your reasons for what you said just before we were interrupted?"

"What has happened here is basic to the entire Fifty Suns' problem," the older woman said coolly. "It is too important to allow any interference. Your husband must be removed from the ship, and you must allow yourself to be conditioned out of love with him until this affair is finally settled. You see that, don't you?"

"No!" the Lady Laurr said stubbornly. "I do not. On what do you base your opinion?"

"There are several notable points," said the psychologist. "One of them is the fact that *you* married him. Madam, you would never have married an ordinary person."

"Naturally," the grand captain spoke proudly. "You yourself have stated that his I.Q.'s, both of them, are greater than mine."

Lieutenant Neslor laughed scathingly. "Since when has I.Q. mattered to you? If that were a reason for recognizing equality, then the royal and noble families of the galaxy would long ago have become saturated with professors and scholars. No, no my captain, there is in a person born to high estate an instinctive sense of greatness which has nothing to do with intelligence or ability. We less fortunate mortals may feel that that is unfair, but there is nothing we can do about it. When his lordship walks into the room, we may dislike him, hate him, ignore him or kowtow to him. But we are never indifferent to him. Captain Maltby has that air. You may not have been consciously aware of it when you married him, but you were, subconsciously."

"But he's only a captain in the Fifty Suns navy," the grand captain protested, "and he was an orphan, raised by the state."

Lieutenant Neslor was cool. "He knows who he is, make no mistake. My only regret is that you married him so swiftly, thus barring me from making a detailed examination of his two minds. I am very curious about his history."

"He has told me everything."

"Noble lady," said the psychologist sharply. "Examine what you are saying. We are dealing with a man whose lowest I.Q. is more than 170. Every word you have spoken about him shows the bias of a woman for her lover. I am not," the older woman continued, "questioning your basic faith in him. As far as I have been able to determine, he is an able and honest man. But your final decisions about the Fifty Suns must be made without reference to your emotional life. Do you see now?"

There was a long pause, and then an almost imperceptible nod. "Put him off," she said in a drab voice, "at Atmion. We must turn back to Cassidor."

Chapter Seventeen

MALTBY stood on the ground, and watched the *Star Cluster* fade into the blue mist of the upper sky. Then he turned, and caught a ground car to the nearest hotel. From there he made his first call. In an hour a young woman arrived, who saluted him stiffly as she came into his presence. But as he stood watching her, some of the hostility went out of her. She came forward, knelt gingerly, and kissed his hand.

"You may rise," Maltby said.

She stood up, and retreated, watching him with alert, faintly amused, faintly defiant gaze.

Maltby felt sardonic about it himself. The decision of generations of Mixed Men that hereditary rulership was the only practical solution to leadership among so many immensely able men had backfired somewhat when Peter Maltby, the son of the last active hereditary leader, had been captured by the Dellians in the same battle that had killed his father. After long consideration, the lesser leaders had decided to reaffirm his rights. They had even begun to believe that it would be of benefit to the Mixed Men to have their leader grow up among the people of the Fifty Suns. Particularly since good behavior on his part and by the other captured, now grown-up children, might be a way of winning back the good opinion of the Fifty Suns people. Some of the older leaders actually considered that the one hope of the race. It was interesting to know that, in spite of Hunston's action, one woman partially recognized his status.

"My situation is this," Maltby said, "I'm wearing a suit which, I am convinced, is tuned to a finder on the

Star Cluster. I want someone to wear it while I go to *the* hidden city."

"I'm sure that can be arranged," she said. "The ship will come at midnight tomorrow to the rendezvous. Can you make it?"

"I'll be there."

She hesitated. "Is there anything else?"

"Yes," said Maltby, "who's backing Hunston?"

"The young men." She spoke without hesitation.

"What about the young women?"

She smiled at that. "I'm here, am I not?"

"Yes, but only with half your heart."

"The other half," she said, unsmiling now, "is with a young man who is fighting in one of Hunston's armies."

"Why isn't your whole heart there?"

"Because I don't believe in deserting a system of government at the first crisis. We chose hereditary leadership for a definite period. We women do not altogether approve of these impulsive adventures, led by adventurers like Hunston, though we recognize that this is a crisis."

"There will be many dead men before this is over," Maltby said gravely, "I hope your young man is not among them."

"Thank you," she said, and went out.

There were nine nameless planets, nine hidden cities where the Mixed Men lived. Like the planets, the cities had no names. They were referred to with a very subtle accent on the article in the phrase *"the* city." *The!* In every case the cities were located underground, three of them beneath great, restless seas, two under mountain ranges, the other four—no one knew.

Maltby had discovered, in his one journey, that no one knew. The outlets were far from the cities, the tunnels that led to them wound so tortuously that the biggest spaceships had to proceed at very low speeds around the curves. The ship that came for Maltby was only ten minutes late. It was operated mostly by women, but there were some older men along, including three of his long-dead father's chief advisers, Johnson, Saunders, and Collings. The last named acted as spokesman.

"I'm not sure, sir," he said, "that you should come to *the* city. There is a certain hostility, even among the women. They are afraid for their sons, husbands and sweethearts, but loyal to them. All the actions of Hunston and the others have been secret. We have had no idea what is going on. There is no information to be had at *the* hidden city."

"I didn't expect there would be," Maltby replied. "I want to give a speech, outlining the general situation as I see it."

Later—when Maltby faced his audience, there was no applause. The twenty thousand people in the massive auditorium heard his words in silence that seemed to grow more intense as he described some of the weapons on the *Star Cluster*.

When he outlined the policies of Imperial Earth with respect to lost colonies like the Fifty Suns, their disapproval was even more evident, but he finished with grim determination: "Unless the Mixed Men can arrive at some agreement with Earth, or discover some means of nullifying the power of Earth, then all the preliminary victories are futile, meaningless and certain to end in disaster. There is no power on the Fifty Suns strong enough to defeat the battleship *Star Cluster*, let alone all the other ships that Earth could send here in an emergency. Therefore—"

He was cut off. All over the great hall, mechanical speakers shouted in unison. "He's a spy for his Earth wife. He never was one of us."

Maltby smiled darkly. So Hunston's friends had decided his sobering arguments might get results, and this was their answer. He waited for the mechanized interruptions to end. But the minutes flew by and the bedlam grew, rather than lessened. The audience was not the kind that approved of noise as a logical form of argument. As Maltby watched, several angry women tore down loud speakers they could reach, but as many of them were in the ceiling, it was not a general solution. The confusion increased.

Hunston and his men must know, Maltby thought

tensely, that they were irritating their followers here. How did they dare take the risk? Only one answer seemed reasonable: They were playing for time. They had something up their collective sleeve, something big, that would overwhelm all irritation and all opposition.

A hand was tugging at his arm. He turned and saw that it was Collings. The old man looked anxious.

"I don't like this," he said, above the uproar. "If they'll go this far, then they might even dare to assassinate you. Perhaps you had better return at once to Atmion, or Cassidor, wherever you wish to go."

Maltby looked thoughtful. "It has to be Atmion," he said finally. "I don't want the people on the *Star Cluster* to suspect that I have been wandering. In one sense, I no longer have any commitments there, but I think the contact might still be valuable."

He smiled wryly, for that was an understatement if there ever was one. It was true that Gloria had been conditioned out of love with him, but he had been left conditioned *in* love with her. No matter how hard he tried he couldn't dismiss the reality of that. "You know how to get in touch with me," he said, "if anything turns up."

That, also, was not amusing. He had a pretty shrewd idea that Hunston would make particularly certain that no information came to *the* hidden city on *the* nameless planet. Just how he was going to obtain information was another matter.

Suddenly he felt completely cast out. Like a pariah, he left the stage. The noise faded behind him.

The days passed; and the puzzling thing to Maltby was that he heard nothing about the *Star Cluster*. For a month of hours, he went aimlessly from city to city; and the only news that came through was of the success of the Mixed Men. Highly colored news it was. Everywhere, the conquerors must have seized radio control; and glowing accounts came of how the inhabitants of the Fifty Suns were wildly acclaiming their new rulers as leaders in the fight against the ship from Imperial Earth. Against the humans whose ancestors, fifteen thousand years before, had massacred all robots they could find, forcing the survivors to flee to this remote cloud of stars.

Over and over, the theme repeated. No "robot"—the word was used—could trust a human being after what had happened in the past. The Mixed Men would save the "robot" world from the untrustworthy human beings and their battleship.

A very unsettling and chilling note of triumph entered the account every time the battleship was mentioned. Maltby frowned over that, not for the first time, as he ate his lunch in an open-air restaurant on the thirty-first day. Soft, though vibrant music, poured over his head from the public announcer system. It was almost literally *over* his head, because he was too intent to be more than dimly aware of outside sound.

One question dominated his thought: What had happened to the *Star Cluster?* Where *could* it be?

Gloria had said: "We shall take immediate action. Earth recognizes no governments by minorities. The Mixed Men will be given democratic privileges and equality, not dominance. That is final."

It was also, Maltby realized, reasonable IF human beings had really gotten over their prejudice against so-called robots. It was a big if; and their prompt unloading of him from the ship proved that it wasn't a settled problem by any means.

The thought ended, as, above him, the music faded out on a high pitched note. The brief silence was broken by the unmistakable voice of Hunston:

"To all people of the Fifty Suns, I make this important announcement: The Earth battleship is a danger no more. It has been captured by a skillful trick of the Mixed Men and it is at Cassidor, where it is even now yielding its many secrets to the technical experts of the Mixed Men. People of the Fifty Suns, the days of strain and uncertainty are over. Your affairs will in future be administered by your kin and protectors, the Mixed Men. As their leader and your leader, I herewith dedicate the thirty billion inhabitants of our seventy planets to the task of preparing for future visitations from the main galaxy, and of insuring that no warship will ever again venture far into the Greater Magellanic Cloud, which we now solemnly proclaim to be our living space, sacred and inviolable forever.

"But that is for the future. For the moment, we the people of the Fifty Suns have successfully circumvented the most hideous danger of our history. A three day celebration is accordingly declared. I decree music, feasting and laughter—"

At first there seemed nothing to think. Maltby walked along a boulevard of trees and flowers and fine homes; and, after a while, his mind tried to form a picture of an invincible battleship captured with all on board—if they were still alive. How had it been done? By all the blackness in space, *how?*

Mixed Men, with their hypnotically powerful double minds, if allowed aboard in sufficient numbers to seize mental control of all high officers, could have done it.

But who would be mad enough to let that first group get into the ship? Until a month ago, the *Star Cluster* had had two protections at least against such a disastrous finale to its long voyage. The first was the ship's able psychologist, Lieutenant Neslor, who would unhesitatingly pry into the brain of every person who entered the ship. The second safeguard was Captain Peter Maltby, whose double brain would instantly recognize the presence of another Mixed Man.

Only, Maltby was not on the ship, but walking along this quiet, magnificent street, consuming himself with amazement and dismay. He was here because—He sighed with sudden immense understanding. So that was why the light-globe had appeared to him, and why Hunston had been so plausible. The man's words had had nothing to do with his intentions. The whole act had been designed to force off the ship the one man who would instantly sense the presence of a Mixed Man. It was difficult to know what he would have done if he had discovered them. To betray one's kin to death for the love of an alien woman, was almost unthinkable. Yet he couldn't have allowed *her* to be captured. Perhaps his course would have been to warn the would-be conquerors to keep away. The choice, forced upon him at the flash moment of attack, would have taxed the logic capacity of his brain.

It didn't matter now. The events had fallen their chance ways without reference to him. He couldn't change the larger aspect of them. The political seizure of the Fifty Suns government, the capture of a mighty battleship, all these were beyond the influence of a man who had been proved wrong by events, and who could now be killed without anybody, even his former supporters, worrying too much about him. It wouldn't do to contact *the* hidden city in this hour of Hunston's triumph.

There remained a fact that he had to do something about. If it were a fact that the *Star Cluster* had been captured, then so had the Right Honorable Gloria Cecily. And the Lady Laurr of Noble Laurr was in addition to all her great titles, Mrs. Peter Maltby. That was the reality. Out of it grew the first purely personal purpose of his lonely life.

Chapter Eighteen

THE naval yard spread before him. Maltby paused on the side-walk a hundred feet from the main officers' entrance, and casually lighted a cigarette. Smoking was primarily a non-Dellian habit; and he had never contracted it. But a man who wanted to get from planet IV of the Atmion sun, to Cassidor VII without going by regular ship needed a flexible pattern of small actions to cover such moments as this.

He lit the cigarette while his gaze took in the gate and the officer in charge of the guard. He walked forward finally with the easy stride of a person with clear conscience. He stood, puffing, while the man, a Dellian, examined his perfectly honest credentials. The casualness was a mask. He was thinking, in a mental sweat: It *would* be a Dellian. With such a man, hypnotism, except under certain conditions of surprise, would be impossible.

The officer broke the silence. "Step over to the postern, captain," he said, "I want to talk to you."

Maltby's primary mind sagged, but his secondary brain grew as alert as steel suddenly subjected to strain. Was this discovery? On the verge of slashing forth with his minds, he hesitated. Wait! he warned himself. Time enough to act if an attempt was made to sound an alarm. He must test to the limit his theory that Hunston wouldn't have had time to close all the gates against him.

He glanced sharply at the other's face. But the typically handsome countenance of a Dellian was typically impassive. If this were discovery, it was already too late for his special brand of hypnotism.

131

The Dellian began in a low voice, without preamble: "We have orders to pick you up, captain."

He paused and stared curiously at Maltby, who probed cautiously with his minds, met an invincible barrier, and withdrew, defeated but nonplussed. So far, there was nothing menacing.

Maltby studied the fellow closely. "Yes?" he said cautiously.

"If I let you in," the Dellian said, "and something happened, say, a ship disappeared, I'd be held responsible. But if I don't let you in, and you just walk away, no one will guess that you've been here." He shrugged and smiled. "Simple, eh?"

Maltby stared at the man gloomily. "Thanks," he said. "But what's the idea?"

"We're undecided."

"About what?"

"About the Mixed Men. This business of their taking over the government is all very well. But the Fifty Suns navy does not forswear, or swear, allegiance in ten minutes. Besides, we're not sure that Earth's offer was not an honest one."

"Why are you telling me this? After all, I am physically a Mixed Man."

The other smiled. "You've been thoroughly discussed in the mess-halls, captain. We haven't forgotten that you were one of us for fifteen years. Though you may not have noticed it, we put you through many tests during that period."

"I noticed," said Maltby, his face dark with memory. "I had the impression that I must have failed the tests."

"You didn't."

There was silence. But Maltby felt a stirring of excitement. He had been so intent on his own troubles that the reaction of the people of the Fifty Suns to cataclysmic political change had scarcely touched him. Come to think of it, he had noticed among civilians the same uncertainty as this officer was expressing.

There seemed little doubt, the Mixed Men had seized control at a beautifully timed psychological moment. But their victory wasn't final. There was still opportunity here for the purposes of others. Maltby said simply, "I want to get to Cassidor to find out what has happened to my wife. How can I manage it?"

"The grand captain of the *Star Cluster* is really your wife! That wasn't propaganda?"

Maltby nodded. "She's really my wife."

"And she married you knowing you were a robot?"

"I spent weeks in the battleship's library," Maltby said, "looking up Earth's version of the massacre of the robots, which took place fifteen thousand years ago. Their explanation was that it was a brief revival in the mass of the people, of old-time race prejudices which as you know, were rooted in fear of the alien and, of course, in pure elemental antipathy. The Dellian was such a superbly handsome being, and with his curious physical and mental powers *seemed* to be superior to naturally born men that, in one jump, the fear became a panicky hate, and the lynchings began."

"What about the non-Dellian?" the officer asked, "who made possible the escape, and yet about whom so little is known?"

Maltby laughed grimly. "That is the cream of the jest. Listen—"

When he had finished his explanation, the officer said blankly, "And do the people of the *Star Cluster* know this?"

"I told them," Maltby said. "They were intending to make the announcement just before the ship went back to Earth."

There was silence. Finally the Dellian said, "What do you think of this business of Mixed Men seizing our government and organizing for war?"

"I'm undecided."

"Like the rest of us."

"What troubles me," said Maltby, "is that there are bound to be other Earth battleships arriving, and some of them at least will not be captured by trickery."

"Yes," said the Dellian, "we've thought of that."

The silence settled, and lasted longer this time before

Maltby brought out his request. "Is there any way that I can get to Cassidor?"

The Dellian stood with closed eyes, hesitating. At last he sighed. "There's a ship leaving in two hours. I doubt if Captain Terda Laird will object to your presence aboard. If you will follow me, captain."

Maltby went through the gate, and into the shadows of the great hangars beyond. There was an odd relaxedness inside him, and he was in space before he realized what it meant. His taut feeling of being alone in a universe of aliens was gone.

Chapter Nineteen

THE darkness beyond the port-holes was soothing to his creative brain. He sat staring into the black ink with its glinting brightnesses that were stars; and felt a oneness. Nostalgic memory came of all the hours he had spent like this when he was a meteorologist in the Fifty Suns navy. Then he had thought himself friendless, cut off from these Dellian and non-Dellian robots by an unbridgeable suspicion.

The truth, perhaps, was that he had grown so aloof that no one had dared to try to close the gap. Now, he knew the suspicion had long dimmed almost to vanishing. Somehow that made the whole Fifty Suns problem his again. He thought; a different approach to the rescue of Gloria was in order. A few hours before the landing, he sent his card to Captain Laird and asked for an interview.

The commanding officer was a non-Dellian, lean and gray and dignified. And he agreed to every word, every detail of Maltby's plan.

"This whole matter," he said, "was threshed out weeks ago, shortly after the Mixed Men seized power. In estimating the total number of a warcraft available to Imperial Earth, we arrived at a figure that was almost meaningless, it was so large.

"It wouldn't be surprising," the officer continued earnestly, "if Earth could detach a warship for every man, woman and child in the Fifty Suns, and not perceptibly weaken the defenses of the main galaxy. We of the navy have been waiting anxiously for Hunston to make a statement either privately or publicly about that. His failure to do so is alarming, particularly as there is some logic in the argument that the first penetration of a new star system like our Greater Magellanic Cloud, would be undertaken on the orders of the central executive."

"It's an Imperial mission," said Maltby, "working on a directive from the Emperor's council."

"Madness!" the Captain muttered. "Our new leaders are madmen." He straightened, shaking his head, as if to clear it of darkness and confusion. He continued in a resonant voice, "Captain Maltby, I think I can guarantee you the full support of the navy in your effort to rescue your wife if . . . if she is still alive."

As he fell through the darkness an hour later, down and down and down, Maltby forced the warming effects of that promise to dim the grim import of the final words. Once, his old sardonicism surged like a stirred fire; and he thought ironically; almost incredible that only a few months had passed since circumstances had made it necessary for Lieutenant Neslor, the *Star Cluster's* psychologist, to force on him an intense emotional attachment for Gloria. The attachment, which, ever since, had been the ruling passion of his life.

She, on the other hand, had fallen in love with him naturally. Which was one of the reasons why their relationship was so precious to him.

The planet below was brighter, larger. A crescent sitting comfortably in space, its dark side sparkling with the silver flashing lights of tens of thousands of towns and cities. That was where he headed, toward the twinkling dark side. He landed in a grove of trees, and he was burying his spacesuit beside a carefully marked tree, when the total blackness struck him.

Maltby felt himself falling over. He hit the ground with a sharp impact, distinctly aware of his consciousness fading out of his mind.

He woke up, amazed; and looked around him. It was still dark. Two of the three moons of Cassidor were well above the horizon, and they hadn't even been in sight when he landed. Their light shed vaguely over the small glade.

It was the same grove of trees. He moved his hands—

and they moved; they were not tied. He sat up, then stood up. He was alone.

There was not a sound, except the faint whispering of wind through the trees. He stood, eyes narrowed, suspicious; then, slowly, he relaxed. He had heard, he remembered suddenly, of unconsciousness like this overwhelming non-Dellians after a long fall through space. Dellians were not affected; and until this instant he had thought Mixed Men were also immune. They weren't. There was no doubt about that. He shrugged, and forgot it. It took about ten minutes to walk to the nearest air stop. Ten minutes later he was in an air center. He knew his way now. He paused in one of the forty entrances and probing briefly with his two minds, satisfied himself that there were no Mixed Men among the masses of people surging toward the various escalators. It was a tiny satisfaction at best. Tiny because he had known Hunston couldn't possibly spare the men for complicated patrol duty. The leader of the Mixed Men could talk as glibly as he pleased about his armies. But Maltby smiled darkly—there was no such force.

The *coup d'etat* that had won Hunston control of the Fifty Suns was a far bolder, more risky accomplishment than was readily apparent. It must have been undertaken with less than a hundred thousand men—and the danger to Peter Maltby would be at the point of disembarkation at the mighty city of Della, Capital of the Fifty Suns.

He had just bought his ticket and was striding toward a fourth level escalator when the woman touched his arm. In a single flash, Maltby had her mind, then as swiftly he relaxed. He found himself staring at Lieutenant Neslor, chief psychologist of the *Star Cluster*.

Maltby set down his cup and stared unsmilingly across the table at the woman psychologist.

"Frankly," he said, "I am not interested in any plan you may have for recapturing the ship. I am in a position where I cannot conscientiously take sides on the larger measures." He paused and studied her curiously, but without any real thought. The emotional life of the middle-aged woman had puzzled him at times. In the past he had wondered if she had used the machines in her laboratories to condition herself against all human feeling. The memory of that thought touched his brain as he sat there. The memory faded. It was information he wanted, not addenda on her character. He said, more coldly, "To my mind, you are responsible for the ignominious capture of the *Star Cluster*, first because it was you, in your scientific wisdom, who had me, a protective force, put off the ship; second, because it was your duty to explore the minds of those who were permitted aboard. I still can't understand how you could have failed."

The woman was silent. Thin and graying at the temples, handsome in a mature fashion, she sat sipping her drink. She met his gaze finally, and said, "I am not going to offer any explanations. Defeat speaks for itself." She broke off, flashed, "You think our noble lady will fall into your arms with gratitude when you rescue her. You forget that she has been conditioned out of love with you, and that only her ship matters to her."

"I'll take my chances on that," he said, "and I'll take it alone. And if we are ever again subject to Earth laws, I shall exercise my legal rights."

Lieutenant Neslor's eyes narrowed. "Oh," she said, you know about that. You did spend a great deal of time in the library, didn't you?"

Maltby said quietly, "I probably know more about Earth laws than any other individual on the *Star Cluster*."

"And you won't even listen to my plan, to use the thousand survivors to help in the rescue?"

"I've told you," he said, "I cannot participate in the larger issues."

The woman stood up. "But you *are* going to try to rescue Lady Gloria?"

"Yes."

She turned without another word, and walked off. He watched her until she disappeared through a distant door.

Chapter Twenty

GRAND CAPTAIN, the Right Honorable Gloria Cecily, the Lady Laurr of Noble Laurr, sat in the throne chair of her reception dais, and listened unsmilingly to the psychologist's report. It was not until the older woman finished that the bleakness of the listener showed abatement. Her voice, however, was sharp as she said, "Then he definitely didn't suspect the truth? He didn't discover that the *Star Cluster* has never been captured. He didn't realize that it was you who made him unconscious when he landed in the grove of trees?"

"Oh, he was suspicious," Lieutenant Neslor said, "but how could he so much as guess the larger truth? In view of our silence, how could he suspect that Hunston's triumphant announcement was only a part of the ever deadlier game he and we are playing, in our attempts to destroy each other? The very fact that Hunston *has* got an Earth battleship makes it particularly impossible for anybody to realize the truth."

The young noblewoman nodded, smiling now. She sat for a moment, proud eyes narrowed with thought, lips parted, gleaming white teeth showing. That had not been the expression on her face when first she had learned that the Mixed Men also had an Earth battleship, and a marvelously new model at that, a ship whose type had been in the design stage for many years. Sitting there, all the knowledge she had on the subject of that new thundership, as it was called in the naval yards, was flashingly reviewed in her mind. How its nine hundred billion separate parts had gone into mass production seventy-five years before, with the expectation that the first ship would

139

be completed at the end of seventy years, and additional ones thereafter on a mass production basis. Very few of the vessels would actually be in service as yet, but somewhere along the line one of them had been stolen.

Her feelings concerning the possession by the Mixed Men of such a battleship had been an imbalance of relief and alarm. Relief that the super-inventions of the Mixed Men were after all only stolen from the main galaxy. And alarm at the implications of such a capture.

What were Hunston's intentions? How *did* he intend to get around the fact that Imperial Earth had more warships than there were men, women and children in the Fifty Suns?

She said slowly, "Undoubtedly the Mixed Men sent a ship to the main galaxy the moment they heard about us; and, of course, if enough of them ever got aboard one of our warships there would be no stopping them." She broke off more cheerfully, "I'm glad that Captain Maltby did not question your account of how you and a thousand other crew members escaped when Hunston made his so-called seizure of the *Star Cluster*. I am not surprised that he refused to have anything to do with your harebrained scheme of recapturing the ship. The important thing is that, under cover of this pretty little story, you learned what we wanted to know: His love fixation for me is driving him to an attempt to board Hunston's battleship. When the indicator we have had pointing at him since he left us at Atmion indicates that he is inside the ship, then we shall act." She laughed, "He's going to be a very surprised young man when he discovers what kind of clothes he is wearing."

Lieutenant Neslor said, "He may be killed."

There was silence, and the faint smile remained on the finely molded face of Lady Laurr.

Lieutenant Neslor said quickly, "Do not forget that your present antagonism towards him is influenced by your present comprehension of how deeply you had previously committed yourself to an emotional attachment."

"It is possible," admitted the grand captain, "that your conditioning was over enthusiastic. Whatever the reason,

I have no desire to feel other than I do now. You may therefore consider this a command: Under no circumstances am I to be reconditioned into my former state. The divorce between Captain Maltby and myself, now that it has taken place, is final. Is that clear?"

"Yes, noble lady."

Here were ships, ships, ships more than Maltby had ever seen in the Cassidor yards. The Fifty Suns navy was undoubtedly being demobilized as fast as the Mixed Men could manage it.

The ships stretched in ranks to the north, to the east, to the south, as far as the eye could see. They lay in their cradles in long, geometric rows. Here and there, surface hangars and repair shops broke that measured rhythm of straight lines. But for the most part the buildings were underground, or rather, under sheeted plains of metal, hidden by a finely corrugated sea of translucent steel alloy.

The Earth battleship lay about four miles from the western entrance. The distance seemed to have no diminishing effect on its size. It loomed colossal on the horizon, overshadowing the smaller ships, dominating the sky and the planet and the sections of the city that spread beyond it. Nothing in Cassidor, nothing in the Fifty Suns system, could begin to approach that mighty ship for size, for complication, for sheer appearance of power.

Even now, it seemed incredible to Maltby that so great a weapon, a machine that could destroy whole planets, had fallen intact into the hands of the Mixed Men, captured by a trick. And yet the very method he had used to free the *Atmion* was evidence that it could be done. With an effort, Maltby drew his mind from that futile contemplation, and walked forward. He felt cold, and steady and determined. The officer at the gate was a pleasant-faced non-Dellian, who took him through, saying: "There is an electronic matter transmitter focused from the ship's hold into the doorway of that building." He motioned a hundred yards ahead and to one side, and continued: "That will get you inside the battleship. Now put this alarm device in your pocket."

Maltby accepted the tiny instrument curiously. It was an ordinary combination sending and receiving tube with a lock button to activate the signal.

"What's this for?" he asked.

"You're heading for the Grand Captain's bridge, are you not?"

Maltby nodded, but there was a thought beginning in his mind; and he did not trust himself to speak. He waited. The man continued: "As soon as you can, make every effort to go over to the control board and nullify energy flows, force connections, automatic screens and so on. Then press the signal."

The thought inside Maltby was an emptiness. He had a sudden sense of walking along the edge of an abyss. "But what's the idea?" he asked blankly.

The answer was quiet, almost cool. "It has been decided," said the young officer, "to try to take the battleship. We got hold of some spare transmitters, and we are ready to put a hundred thousand men aboard in one hour, from the various concentration centers. Whatever the result, in the confusion of the attack, your chances of escaping with your wife will be augmented."

He broke off crisply, "You understand your instructions?"

Instructions! So that was it. He was a member of the Fifty Suns navy, and they took it for granted that he was subject to orders without question. He wasn't of course. As hereditary leader of the Mixed Men, who had sworn allegiance to the Fifty Suns, and married the representative of Imperial Earth, his loyalty was a problem in basic ethics.

The wry thought came to Maltby that only an attack by the survivors of the *Star Cluster* was needed now. Led by Lieutenant Neslor, their arrival would just about make a perfect situation for a man whose mind was running around in circles, faster and faster every minute. He needed time to think, to decide. And fortunately, the time was going to be available. *This* decision didn't have to be made here and now. He would take the alarm device—

and sound it or not according to his determination at the moment. He slipped the instrument into his pocket and said quietly, "Yes, I understand my instructions."

Two minutes later he was inside the battleship.

Chapter Twenty-One

THE storeroom, in which Maltby found himself, was deserted. The pleasurable shock of that staggered him. It seemed almost too good to be true. His gaze flashed over the room. He couldn't remember ever having been in it when he was aboard the *Star Cluster*. But then, he had never had any reason to wander all over the mighty ship. Nor, for that matter, had he had time.

He walked swiftly over to the inter-room transmitter, reached up to press the toucher that would enable him to step from the hold into the grand captain's bridge. But at the last instant, his fingers actually on the toucher, he hesitated.

It had been wise, of course, to do everything boldly. The whole history of warfare taught that planned boldness, tempered with alertness, weighed heavily in the balance of victory. Only, he hadn't really planned. Consciously he let his secondary, Dellian mind—tilt—forward. He stood very still, mentally examining his actions from the moment that Hunston had projected the globe of force into his bedroom, through the trip to Cassidor, the talk he had had with Lieutenant Neslor, and the suddenly announced attack plan of the Fifty Suns navy.

Thinking about it, it struck him sharply that the overall, outstanding effect was of complication. The Dellian part of his brain, with its incisive logic, usually had little difficulty organizing seemingly unrelated facts into whatever unity was innate in them. Yet now, it was slow in resolving the details. It took a moment to realize why. Each was a compound of many smaller facts, some of them partially resolvable by deduction, others though

144

undoubtedly there, refused to come out of the mist. There was no time to think about it now. He had decided to enter the grand captain's cabin and there was only one way to do it. With an abrupt movement, he pressed the toucher. He stepped through into a brightly lighted room. A tall man was standing about a dozen feet from the transmitter, staring at it. In his fingers he held an In-no gun.

It was not until the man spoke that Malby recognized Hunston. The leader of the Mixed Men said in a ringing voice: "Welcome, Captain Maltby, I've been waiting for you."

For once, boldness had failed.

Maltby thought of snatching his own In-no gun from its holster. He thought of it but that was all. Because, first, he glanced over the control board, to the section that governed the automatic defenses of the interior of the ship. A single light glowed there. He moved his hand slowly. The light flickered, showing awareness of him. He decided not to draw his weapon. The possibility that that light would be on had made it highly inadvisable to enter the main bridge, weapon in hand.

Maltby sighed and gave his full attention to the other. It was several months since he had seen Hunston. Like all men with Dellian blood in them, like Maltby himself, Hunston was a superbly well-proportioned being. His mother must have been a blonde and his father a very dark brunette, because his hair had come out the curious mixture of gold and black that always resulted from such a union. His eyes were gray-blue. In their earlier meeting Hunston had been slenderer, and somehow immature in spite of his confidence and personality. That was all gone now. He looked strong and proud, and every inch a leader of men. He said without preamble:

"Briefly the facts are these: This is not the *Star Cluster*. My statement about that was political maneuvering. We captured this battleship from a naval yard in the main galaxy. A second battleship, now in process of being captured, will soon be here. When it arrives, we shall engage the *Star Cluster* in a surprise attack."

The change of Maltby's status from rescuer to dupe was

swift as that. One instant he was a man tensed with determination, geared to withstand any danger; the next a fool, his purpose made ludicrous.

He said: "B-but—"

It was a sound, not a reaction. A word expressing blankness, a thoughtless state, which preceded the mind storm, out of which grew understanding. Before Maltby could speak, Hunston said:

"Someone advised us that you were coming. We assume it was your wife. We assume furthermore that there is hostile purpose behind every move she is making. Accordingly, we prepared for any emergency. There are ten thousand Mixed Men inside this ship. If your arrival here is to be a signal for an attack, it will have to be well organized indeed to surprise us."

Once more, there were too many facts. But after a moment, Maltby thought of the Fifty Suns navy men, waiting to enter the battleship, and flinched. He parted his lips to speak, and closed them again as his Dellian mind projected into his primary the memory of his meeting with Lieutenant Neslor. The logic capacity of that second mind was on a plane that had no human parallel. There was a flashing connection made between the meeting with the psychologist and the blackness that had struck him down at the moment of his landing on Cassidor. Instantly, that marvelous secondary brain examined a thousand possibilities, and since it had enough clues at last, came forth with the answer.

The suit he was wearing!!! He must have been made unconscious, in order to substitute it for the one he *had* been wearing. Any minute, any *second*, it would be activated. Sweating, Maltby pictured the resulting clash of titans: Ten thousand Mixed Men versus a major portion of the crew of the *Star Cluster* versus one hundred thousand men of the Fifty Suns navy.

If only that last group would wait for his signal, then he could save them by not sounding it. Sharp consciousness came that he ought to speak, but first—

He must find out if the suit had been energized.

He put his arm behind his back, and pushed his hand

cautiously *into* his back. It went in four inches, six inches; and still there was only emptiness. Slowly, Maltby withdrew his arm.

The suit was activated all right.

Hunston was saying: "Our plan is to destroy the *Star Cluster*, then Earth itself."

"W-what?" said Maltby.

He stared. He had a sudden feeling that he had not heard correctly. He echoed, his voice loud in his own ears, "Destroy Earth!"

Hunston nodded coolly. "It's the only logical course. If the one planet is destroyed, on which men know of the *Star Cluster's* expedition to the Lesser Magellanic Cloud, then we shall have time to expand, to develop our civilization; and eventually, after a few hundred years of intensive breeding of Mixed Men, we shall have enough population to take over the control of the main galaxy itself."

"But," Maltby protested, "Earth is the center of the main galaxy. All the government is there, the Imperial symbol. It's the *head* of the planets of 3000 million suns. It—" he stopped. The fear that came was all the greater because it was not personal.

"Why, you madman!" he cried angrily. "You can't do a thing like that. It would disorganize the entire galaxy."

"Exactly," Hunston nodded with satisfaction. "We would definitely have the time we need. Even if others knew of the *Star Cluster* expedition, no one would connect it with the catastrophe, and no other expedition would be sent."

He paused, then continued, "As you see, I have been very frank with you. And you will not have failed to note that our entire plan depends on whether or not we can first destroy the *Star Cluster*. In this," he finished quietly, "we naturally expect the assistance of the hereditary leader of the Mixed Men."

Chapter Twenty-Two

THERE was silence in the great room. The bank on bank of control board remained impassive, except for the solitary anti-light that glowed like a faint beacon from its deep-inset tube. Standing there, Maltby grew aware of a thought. It had only an indirect relation to the request Hunston had just made, and it wasn't new. He tried to fight it, but it remained strong, and grew stronger, a developing force in his mind. It was the conviction that he would yet have to take sides in this struggle of three powerful groups. He couldn't allow Earth to be destroyed!

With a terrible effort, he finally forced the thought aside, and looked at Hunston. The man was staring at him with narrowed-eyed anxiety that abruptly startled Maltby. He parted his lips to make a sardonic comment about a usurper who had the gall to ask help from the man he was striving to displace.

But Hunston spoke first: *"Maltby—what is the danger? What is their plan in having you come here? You must know by this time."*

Almost, Maltby had forgotten about that. Once more he was about to speak. But this time he stopped himself. There was another thought forming in the back of his mind. It had been there for many months, and in its more detailed conception it was actually his solution to the whole Fifty Suns problem. In the past, the knowledge that the solution required one man to convince three groups, actually to control the three hostile groups at a given hour, and to force them to yield to his will, had made the whole idea ridiculous and impractical.

148

Now, in one mental jump, he saw how it could be done. But hurry, hurry! Any instant, the suit he was wearing would be used. "It's this room!" he said violently. "If you value your life, get out of it at once."

Hunston stared at him, bright eyed. He seemed unafraid. He asked in an interested tone: "This room is the danger point because you're in it?"

"Yes," said Maltby, and held his arms out slightly, and his head up, so that the energy of Hunston's In-no gun would not hit him. His body tensed for the run forward.

Instead of shooting, Hunston frowned. "There's something wrong," he said. "Naturally, I wouldn't leave you in charge of the control room of this battleship. Accordingly, you're practically asking me to kill you. It's obvious that if you're in danger, then you must die. Too obvious." He added sharply, "That anti-light watching you—the moment I fire, its automatic defenses are nullified; and you can use a gun too. Is that what you're waiting for?"

It was.

All Maltby said was, "Get out of this room. Get out, you fool!"

Hunston did not move, but some of the color had faded from his cheeks. He said: "The only danger we've been able to imagine is if somehow they managed to get a *Star Cluster* transmitter aboard." He stared at Maltby. "We haven't been able as yet to figure out how these transmitters work, but we do know this: There is no liaison between the transmitters of one ship and another. They're tuned differently, and set. No amount of manipulation can change them, once completed. But YOU must have had opportunity to learn the secret of their operation. Tell me."

Tell me! It was clear now that he would have to attack in spite of the anti-light. That meant muscles only, which needed a fractional surprise. Starting to tell might do the trick.

But what an odd irony that Hunston and his technical experts had correctly reasoned out the exact nature of the danger. And yet now Huntson, standing in front of a man who was wearing a suit of clothes, both the back and front of which were transmitters, did not suspect.

Maltby said, "Transmitters work in much the same way that the first Dellian robots were made, only they use the original components. The robot constructors took an electronic image of a human being, and constructed what was supposed to be an exact duplicate from organic matter. Something was wrong, of course, because the Dellians never were duplicates of the original human beings, and there were even physical differences. Out of the difference grew the hatred that eventually resulted in the "robot" massacres of fifteen thousand years ago.

"But never mind that. These matter transmitters reduce the body to an electronic flow, and then rebuild the body with the aid of tissue restoration processes. The process has become as simple as turning on a light and—"

It was at that point that Maltby launched his attack. The awful fear that Hunston would aim at his feet, arms, or head, ended. Because in that ultimate moment, the man hesitated and like a thousand million men before him, was lost. The In-no gun did flash, as Maltby grabbed at the wrist of the hand that held it. But the fire sprayed harmlessly against the impregnable floor. And then the gun clattered out of the fight.

"You scoundrel!" Hunston gasped. "You knew I wouldn't fire on the hereditary leader of the Mixed Men. You traitor—"

Maltby had known nothing of the kind. And he did not waste time in consideration of it. Hunston's voice stopped because Maltby had his head in a vicelike grip, and was pulling it towards and *into* his chest. The surprise of that must have been staggering. For a vital moment Hunston ceased his struggling. During that moment, Maltby stuffed him through the transmitter, seemingly right into his own body.

Even as the last squirming foot was shoved out of sight, Maltby was tearing at the fasteners of the suit. He rolled the suit down, so that the transmitter surfaces faced one against the other.

Frantically, he climbed all the way out of the suit and,

racing over to the control board, adjusted the anti-light to work for *him*, and made a dozen other adjustments that he knew about. A minute later, the ship was his.

There remained the necessity of telling the three groups *his* decision. And there remained—Gloria.

Chapter Twenty-Three

THE hearing was held on the tenth day before the captains in session aboard the *Star Cluster*. There must have been preliminary by-play, because by the time Maltby entered she was already there sitting with stiff face and lips, staring straight ahead. Looking at her, Maltby guessed that she had made a last minute effort to prevent the hearing from taking place, and had failed.

Maltby sat down in the place indicated by one of the officers, and waited to be called. He was just a little tense, but not unhappy. He expected that he would have to put up a very good argument to win, but the prize was worth all the effort and thought he had already put into the fight, and that he had yet to put into it.

Out of the corner of one eye, he glanced at the prize—and glanced hastily away again when her own gaze met his squarely, with intermingled sparks and icy gleamings almost leaping from her eyes to his. She stood up, and came over to him.

"Captain Maltby," she said in a low tone, "I beg you not to force this issue."

"Your excellency," said Maltby, "you are almost as attractive to me when you are angry as when you are—acquiescent."

"That is a vulgar remark, and I shall never forgive you for it." Her tone was hot.

"I am sorry if you think that I am vulgar," he said. "This was not always your feeling, as you may recall."

A flush touched those handsome cheeks. She said stiffly, "I do not desire to recall what now seems unpleasant to me. If you were a gentleman, you would not force this issue."

"I hope," said Maltby, "that you will continue to regard me as a gentleman in the accepted meaning of the term. But I do not see how this has anything to do with our affection for each other."

"No gentleman would try to enforce affection, where it is not reciprocated."

Maltby said, "My only desire is to re-establish natural affection that was forcibly altered."

She stared at him with fists clenched, almost as if she planned to hit him. She said abruptly: "Oh, you damned space lawyer. I wish—I wish I'd never let you into our libraries."

Maltby smiled. "Gloria, my dear," he said in a confidential tone, "I hear you're a pretty good space lawyer yourself. I'm going to make a wager with you."

"I do not gamble." Coldly.

It was such an outrageous statement, after all that had happened, that Maltby was momentarily silenced by the sheer extravagance of it. Then he smiled again, more broadly. "My dear," he said, "the fact is that you have the knowledge that can win you this case. My wager is that basically you want me to win, and so you won't remember the particular argument that can win for you."

"No such argument exists," she said. "We both know the law; and you are deliberately tormenting me with this kind of talk."

Suddenly, there were tears in her eyes. "Please, Peter," she begged, "drop this case. Let me go free."

Maltby hesitated, startled by the intensity of her appeal. But he had no intention of giving up. This woman had given herself to him without reservations on the planet of S Doradus. If, after being released from the artificial psychological pressure, she still didn't want him, then she was free. He said earnestly. "My dear, what are you afraid of—yourself? Remember, the choice will be yours afterwards. Right now, you think you're going to choose me, and at the moment you abhor the idea. Once you're freed of the artificial psychological pressure you may feel that you do want the marriage to continue."

"Never. Don't you realize I would have the memory of this period, the memory of being forced? Don't you see that?"

He did, suddenly. All at once he saw that he had been looking at this affair from the viewpoint of a man. Women were different. They had to feel the need for a marriage partner without any slightest vestige of coercion. It was a startling vision for him, because he had been tense and intent. And still he could not bring himself to say the words that would release her.

Sitting there, his mind went back over the events of the past ten days. They had been great days for him. For billions of people had come to agreements on the basis of solutions proposed by himself. The swiftest to accept were the Dellians and non-Dellians. When the news was broadcast that the *Star Cluster* had not been captured by the Mixed Men, and that Earth continued to offer its original guarantees with slight modification, the governments of the Fifty Suns publicly proclaimed agreement.

Maltby had been a little disappointed in the reaction to what he regarded as sensational news. The information —which he had gathered from the battleship's library— that the non-Dellians were NOT humanoids or robots by any extension of the word, but descendants of human beings who had helped the original humanoids to escape, seemed to have no effect. He could only wonder if perhaps too many other things held the attention of people. It was reasonable to hope that there would be a long-run favorable reaction. The non-Dellians would feel a greater kinship with other human beings. The Dellians, realizing that human beings had long ago pretended to be robots for the sake of subsequent generations, might well feel that human beings could be worthwhile folk.

The problem of the Mixed Men had been a little more difficult to resolve. With their volatile leader Hunston a prisoner, the great majority of them seemed to accept the defeat, and agreed to accept Maltby's solution. In his announcement to the Hidden Cities, he was quite blunt.

Having chosen war, they were fortunate to be given a status of equality within the government of the Fifty Suns. All the ships of the main galaxy would be warned against their tactics, and for many years Mixed Men would be required to wear identifying marks. However, Dellians would be allowed to marry non-Dellians, and the couple would no longer be forbidden to have children by the cold-pressure system. Since the child resulting from such a union would invariably be a Mixed Man, there would be over a period of many generations an increase in the number of Mixed Men. If this meant that the mutation would gradually dominate by legal and natural developments, Earth was quite prepared to accept the situation. The laws governing such possibilities were liberal and far-seeing. Fundamentally, only aggression was prohibited.

Remembering all these things, Maltby smiled wryly. All problems were solved but his own. He was still sitting there, undecided when the meeting was called to order.

Three hours later, after a brief discussion among the judges, Captain Rutgers read the decision. It had been hastily written out, and the officer read it out in a sonorous voice:

"The law," he said, "relating to the reintegration of artificially imposed psychological pressure does not apply to Captain Maltby, a non-citizen of Imperial Earth at the time he was conditioned. It does apply to the Lady Gloria, a citizen born."

He went on: "Since Captain Maltby has been made permanent agent to Earth for the Fifty Suns, and since this is the Lady Gloria's last trip into space on a warship, no geographical barriers exist to a continuation of the marriage."

He concluded: "It is accordingly ordered that the Lady Gloria be given the necessary treatment to return her to her former condition of loving affection for her husband."

Maltby took one quick look at Gloria, saw that there were tears in her eyes, and then he stood up. "Your excellencies," he said, "I wish to make a request."

Captain Rutgers indicated that he had the floor. Maltby was momentarily silent. Finally, swallowing a little, he said: "I wish to free my wife from the necessity of undergoing such treatment—on one condition."

"What is the condition?" One of the woman captains asked the question, quickly.

"The condition," said Maltby, "is that at a place of my choosing she allow me forty-eight hours to win her back. If at the end of that time she still feels as she does now, I shall ask that execution of the judgment be indefinitely postponed."

The woman glanced over at her superior. "That seems fair enough, Gloria."

"It's ridiculous," said the Grand Captain of the *Star Cluster*, her color high.

This time it was Maltby who walked over to her. He bent down, and said in a low voice: "Gloria, this is your second chance. After all, you didn't take the first one, as I predicted."

"There was no first one. The decision that has been arrived at here was inevitable, and you know it." She avoided his direct gaze; so it seemed to Maltby.

"It's a basic law of marriage, older than space travel, as old as human history."

She was not avoiding his gaze now. Her eyes stared at him, a dawning understanding in them. "Why, of course," she said, "How could I have forgotten?"

She half-rose to her feet, as if she would still present the argument. Slowly, she sank down again. She said: "What makes you think that you and I cannot have children?"

"No marriage between a human being and a Mixed Man has ever produced a child without artificial aids."

"But with the cold pressure system—"

"No one can be forced to use it," said Maltby. He broke off patiently: "Gloria, you can't escape the fact that this possibility was available to you at any time till the decision was rendered. It's the oldest, and for periods in history it was the only, permitted reason for breaking up a marriage. No one argues with it. It's final. And yet, you sat here fighting to get out of our marriage, and didn't think of it. I regard that as a complete vindication of my feeling that basically you want and need to be married to me. All *I* want is a chance for us to be alone together, and now I have the right to ask it."

She said slowly: "This forty-eight hours that you want us to spend together, where—"

She stopped, her eyes widening. She breathed heavily. "Why, that's ridiculous. I refuse to be a party to such a naively romantic notion. Besides, S Doradus is too far out of the way."

Over her shoulder, Maltby saw that Lieutenant Neslor had come into the room. He gave her a quick, seeking glance, and found her eyes waiting for his. She inclined her head ever so slightly. Whereupon, Maltby lowered his gaze again upon Gloria. He felt no shame for the deal he had made with the woman psychologist to make her readjustments the moment the judgment was in. This tense, proud young woman needed the feeling of natural affection, needed it more perhaps than anyone else in the ship. It was a fact which Lieutenant Neslor had realized as well as he did; and her cooperation had been immediately available. Knowing that she had already been reconditioned out of her dislike of him—though it would require a little time to take effect—he said:

"The planet of S Doradus where we were marooned is only eighteen hours from here. We can take a lifeboat, and later rejoin the *Star Cluster* without interfering with its movements."

She said stingingly: "What do you expect me to do there—fall into your arms?"

"Yes." His voice was steady. "Yes, I do."

THE END

(please turn page)

ROBERT A. HEINLEIN